HABANA LIBRE

HABANA
LIBRE

A NOVELLA
TIM WENDEL

CITYLIT
PRESS

Baltimore, Maryland

Library of Congress Control Number: 2012956266
ISBN 978-1-936328-14-7

CityLit Project is a 501(c)(3) Nonprofit Organization
Federal Tax ID Number: 20-0639118

Printed in the United States of America, First Edition/1p
Editor: Gregg Wilhelm
Book Design: Nathan Rosen
University of Baltimore, MA in Publications Design, 2014
Front Cover Image: AP Images/Ramon Espinosa

CityLit Press is the imprint of nonprofit CityLit Project,
Baltimore's literary arts center.

CITYLIT
PRESS

c/o CityLit Project
120 S. Curley Street
Baltimore, MD 21224
410.274.5691
www.CityLitProject.org
info@citylitproject.org
CityLit Project's offices are located in the School of Communications Design at
the University of Baltimore. For information about UB's MFA in Creative Writing
and Publishing Arts, named one of the country's most distinctive programs by
Poets & Writers magazine, please visit www.ubalt.edu.

DEDICATION

In memory of Eric Wendel, John Douglas, and Bill Glavin.
For Jacqueline, Sarah, and Chris.

TABLE OF CONTENTS

HABANA LIBRE

CUBA, 1999

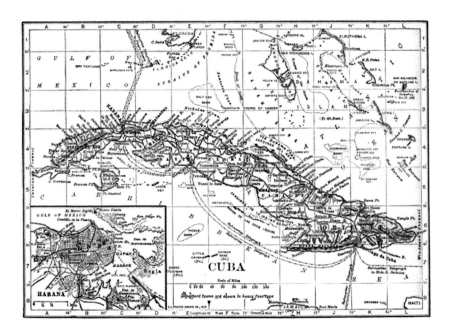

ONE

AS SOON AS PABLO ORTIZ LLANES cleared the breakwater, he realized that the ocean swells were much larger than they appeared from shore. He let out the sheets, letting the sails flap in the wind, just as the old man had taught him not so long ago, but his efforts failed to significantly slow the Hobie Cat down.

It's okay, the boy thought to himself. Such strong winds will carry me that much faster across the Straits of Florida.

But Pablo could feel the panic rising up from his belly, making it more difficult to breath, to concentrate. The beach forecast back at Cayo Coco hadn't called for this much wind. He tacked into the worst of it and for a moment he feared that the rigging, the aluminum mast and the metal shrouds that held it in place would tumble down upon him. The boat stalled atop another towering wave. "In irons"—that's what the old man had called it. By the time Pablo remembered the term, the waves had broken hard across the bows and driven the rear of the Hobie down into the water. A sheet of water raced across the canvas deck that stretched between the craft's two hulls.

Desperate to get the Hobie moving again, moving in any direction, Pablo pulled in on the jib sheet as the mainsail continued to flap crazily in the wind. Head down, so he wouldn't be struck by the metal boom, Pablo felt the boat finally lurch forward. He sailed over the next wave and was borne aloft for enough precious seconds that he had time to fear the fall to earth. And here it came, the twin bows' turn to be buried in the churning waters. As the boat struggled to remain afloat, Pablo saw that he had only one choice: To turn tail and head back to shore. The storm was still building, just playing with him. It was only a matter of time until a wave became too big for the Hobie. Perhaps it would crack one of the hulls below the waterline, that or really bring down the rigging. In any case, it would be a blow from which he couldn't recover.

First, Pablo had to get the big sail down. With one hand on the tiller, Pablo sprawled face-first across the canvas and lifted the main halyard from its jam cleat. The big sail fell in protest, and the boom gave Pablo a nasty knock on the back of his left knee. For a moment, he lost hold of the tiller and the Hobie spun off from the wind. He reached back for the sliver of wood that connected to the rudder beneath the waves. Without somebody at the helm, the small craft became like a crazed beast, ready to run away into the darkness. There, he had the tiller now and pulled it toward him. Down below the waterline, the rudder felt as if it could snap off at any moment. With his other arm, Pablo pulled the rest of the mainsail down and tried to still the fabric by shoving it under his wet legs.

In front of him appeared the wide golden beach, the pride of Cayo Coco. Everything was happening too fast. He needed to bring the Hobie safely through the ragged surf line. If a wave took him sidewise, the boat would roll and break apart on the shore. Needing more speed to maneuver, Pablo pulled in the jib and steered a course across the next bank of fast-moving waves. When those broke past him, he let out the jib sheet and turned directly toward the shore. The next set of waves rose up underneath him and drove the front end of the Hobie down into the water. If it became too shallow too quickly, the bows could catch and send him pinwheeling into the shore. But on this night God was good, and he slid like a tourist on a boogie board safely up the white sand.

Only then did he see that someone had been watching. She was in the water alongside him. Amazingly, she was helping him guide the Hobie back into the quiet lagoon with the rest of the rental fleet from Cayo Coco. It was Pilar Silva, one of the lead dancers in the nightly floor show.

"I tried," Pablo said and immediately regretted such words.

For this Pilar was a beauty. The showgirl who was front and center with her group—the better to show off her eloquent carriage, full breasts, and knowing smile. In fact, she was smiling at him now. She had seen the three plastic jugs of water and the cooler of food that were tied down to the canvas deck.

"I'm impressed," Pilar said, "with your ingenuity."

"What are you doing down here?" Pablo demanded.

But she only smiled and turned her attention back to the boat.

Beyond them the two main structures of the Cayo Coco resort—the casino and the main ballroom, where Pilar danced—glowed in a soft yellow light. Pablo so loved to steal into the big house for the closing dance numbers. He had been there last week when Jorge and Livan had tried out their new comedy routine.

"How many are here from Canada?" Jorge had asked and, of course, about half the place dutifully raised their hands.

"How many from Germany?" Jorge continued while Livan peered out into the crowd that filled the resort ballroom, a hand shading his eyes from the bright spotlight, as if he was truly counting each and every one.

"Colombia? How about Mexico? Venezuela? Japan?"

And so it went until Jorge named about every country under the sun. Nepal and Mongolia got a good laugh. That night there had even been a table of Americans sitting down front, and Livan had them stand up to acknowledge a warm, standing ovation. It made you wish that the politicians in Washington could have seen that.

On and on the list of countries went, and Pablo remembered that Pilar and the other dancers had to hold the pose for so long. Their arms were still out at their sides—palms up to the heavens. The ostrich feathers from the headdress had to be tickling the tips of the nose. He saw the sheen of perspiration growing cold on their foreheads.

"And how many are here from Russia?"

That question was followed by the longest pause of the night. Excruciatingly long. So long that people didn't know whether to laugh or keep quiet in case the authorities were somehow listening in on this moment, too. Livan continued to peer out into the darkness, like he half-expected Vladimir Putin himself to come walking through the main door separating the ballroom from the hotel lobby.

When nobody raised their hand, Jorge asked again, "Who's here from Russia?"

Still, nobody responded and the two comedians in their white tuxes held the moment even a beat longer, squeezing every bit of delight, confusion, and uncertainty out of the crowd. They held it and held it until Livan delivered the punch-line, "What? They've already left?"

The drummer rattled off a quick rat-a-tat-tat. Of course, he was in on the whole setup. And then the room finally exploded into laughter. Such sweetness washed over everyone, and even Pablo had to agree that it was a good joke.

"Come, we must hurry," Pilar said, glancing back at the grand ballroom, where the joke had happened. Nobody was alone, or at least unobserved, for long at Cayo Coco.

Together, he and the showgirl waded into the lagoon and slid the Hobie Cat into its berth. Pilar came alongside him and helped him begin to tie down the lines. That's when it struck Pablo how close he'd come to drowning, out there in the waves. The old man had warned him that the sea could take a man any time it wanted. Weather reports weren't worth a damn. Sometimes, like on a night like tonight, the sea hid malice in its heart.

With shaking hands, Pablo tried to finish tying the half-hitch around the mooring post. But it was no good. Here he was breaking down right in from of this woman. But instead of being embarrassed by his outburst, Pilar brought him to her chest, like a big sister, and Pablo rested there, for a moment, upon that glorious bosom.

"Next time you try," she said, "maybe I'll go with you."

"I'm not trying again," Pablo said, pulling away. "You have my promise about that."

"No, you'll try again," Pilar replied. "I can see it in your eyes. You nearly slipped away from here and you won't forget that. I know I couldn't forget that."

They had almost stowed away the last of the gear when Asafa came down the boardwalk. He wore a poncho and it was as if the skies had been waiting for his arrival, for on cue the heavens opened up, and soon Pablo and the showgirl were drenched to the bone.

"What are you two doing?" Asafa said in a voice as angry as the stormy weather.

Pablo kept his head down, finishing the work. Pilar stared up defiantly at the boss man and then back to Pablo. She waited for him to say something to Asafa. Act like a man. But the situation had made Pablo mute.

"We almost lost it," Pilar began to tell Asafa.

Pablo realized that whatever Pilar said now had to become the truth and he silently prayed that she sold it as hard she did anything on stage. He had seen how she could focus on one gentleman, look him in the eye, and make him believe that she was something dropped to earth by God almighty himself. A beauty that only spoke the truth.

"If it wasn't for Pablo, you would have lost your new toy," Pilar said. The rainwater glistened on her defiant face.

"He should have called for security," Asafa said. "That's the correct procedure."

"He cried out and I was the only one to hear him," Pilar said. God, she was so beautiful, refusing to be bullied. "Now stop making him shit in his pants and start helping us. I don't know how new this stupid boat is, I don't care how much it costs, but it would have been lost in this storm. It was pulled free from the dock and floating out into the surf. You need better rope to harness this one."

"Is that true?" Asafa bellowed, still looking down on them, not raising a finger to help.

The boss man tried to keep them frightened, but Pablo sensed that his voice had softened, just a touch. He was like any man with a problem. He wanted to believe the lie. He wanted to believe the beautiful woman.

"Is that true?" Asafa repeated.

Reluctantly, Pablo peered up at him, still knee-deep in the sloshing water. The boy of barely sixteen nodded and left the next move to Asafa. The boss man was like a big cat: Dangerous, with sharp claws, but he didn't like to be out in the rain.

"All right," Asafa said. "Tie it down—tight this time."

With that he turned and walked away, his steps echoed up the boardwalk.

"Thank you," Pablo whispered.

His chin again sank to his chest. Pilar reached over and raised it back to the land of the living, with a single finger under the chin.

"We'll talk more about this," she smiled. "Much more."

TWO

OMAR SILVA KNEW HE WAS A FOOL to go out of his way to pass the Habana Libre hotel. Too often the detour put him behind a "camel"—the commuter vehicles that looked something a madman had dreamed up. The meat-end of a bus was placed atop flatbed and pulled around by semi-truck's cab. Omar had been to other places in the world—Tennessee in the United States for exhibition games, the last world tournament in Beijing—and he had never seen a contraption as strange as the Cuban camel. He heard they were havens for pickpockets. People carried their money inside their socks, hidden in their shoes, and Omar vowed he would never ride in such a vehicle. After all, he had just been given a refurbished Chevy, a gift from the Baseball Federation for his superb play in the recent Olympics.

Too often when he passed by the Libre, in Havana's west end, he found himself stopped at an intersection next to one of the camels. My God, the way the thing towered into the sky. The poor people wedged on board would peer down at him. Omar was careful never to make eye contact, even when he was often recognized and somebody would call out his name. In the ballpark, he would turn and smile. But not here. Not next to a camel.

But soon enough he would be able to pull ahead, his eyes focused at the off-white monolith. The Libre was still one of the newest-looking buildings in Havana, but that wasn't saying much. If it was up to Fidel, he would have let the whole city, once pride of the Caribbean, fall to dust.

As Omar drew closer, slowing until the horns blared around him and his eyes reluctantly returned to the road, he couldn't believe how the time had already begun to flee from them. Only six weeks ago, he and Pilar had been married at the Libre. While the blessed event would be forever enshrined by photographs of that day and the slivers of memory in his head, even Omar had to admit his marriage had changed a great deal since that blessed day.

How his wife talked now. He blamed it on her return to work at the Cayo Coco. The place had too many tourists. They had to be the ones who put such notions in her head. Why couldn't she have stayed the same? He would always remember how beautiful she had been the morning after the wedding, their first day as man and wife together.

Omar had awoken early and moved to the wicker chair in the corner, in the shadows, to watch her sleep. She had wrapped herself in a single sheet and right then and there Omar decided that no woman was as beautiful as his wife. Pilar seemingly slept without a care in the world. No twitches or soft groans in her sleep. One can say that many women are pretty or bold or interesting, in some basic way, but few of them are truly beautiful.

What a week it had been. The previous Sunday Omar had nearly led Team Cuba past the Baltimore Orioles. The major leaguers from El Norte had been lucky. In their hearts, they had to admit this. To win only 3-2 in eleven innings. A rematch had been scheduled for next month in the United States. Some city called Baltimore. But in his heart Omar would have liked nothing more than to stay there, in the suite at the Libre, and gaze upon his wife. Guard her against all evil and temptation.

That morning Omar had walked out onto the hotel balcony. Below him, the streets of Havana fanned out like crooked fingers, reaching the Malecon seawall and a calm sea. A yellow biplane was the only thing in the cloudless sky, and he watched as it headed north toward the Straits of Florida.

The streets below appeared deserted at first glance. But then Omar saw the bicycles, colored dark-green or dirty brown, swirling like flocks of birds lost upon the earth. In the mornings they filled the wide boulevards shaded by the towering royal palm trees. Many of the traffic lights were turned off years ago. There was no point to having them anymore. The bicycles, imported from China for tons of unrefined Cuban sugar, could go anywhere they wanted.

Their wedding ceremony had been in the Habana Libre ballroom, two flights up from the lobby. Omar had watched how Pilar had carried on when her Uncle Luis arrived. The man had a hand in everything and Pilar held him so close. She hugged him to her chest and let him linger for a long moment. Why not, right? After all, only her Uncle Luis, with his party connections and a hand in the tourist money coming in from Canada and South America and everywhere but the United States, could have arranged such a grand wedding. While his friends had married in white chapels in the middle of banana plantations or, at best, in the stone cathedral in Old Havana, he and Pilar had been married here, in the city's Western Addition, in the shadow of the old hotels and what used to be the grand casinos.

"My, my," Uncle Luis had chuckled as he rose from Pilar's embrace, his cheeks flushed and his smoke-blue eyes wide and dancing, "and to think, Pilar, I used to hold you on my knee. Look at you now."

Omar remembered that Pilar had loved everything about the Libre. How a terrycloth robe, with the HL monogram on the chest pocket, hung in the closet for every guest. For once they had made love decently, not scrambling in the back of an old car or in the team hotel when his roommate, Carmelo, was out getting drunk.

She was just awakening when a knock came on the door to the suite. Omar opened it to find a bellboy with their breakfast, compliments of the management. The eggs were firm and warm. The toast glowed with the sheen of melted butter. Real butter.

"Señor Silva, checkout time is 1 p.m.," the boy said in a low voice, so trying to be deferential.

Omar had waved him off. He knew what time checkout was. He would be gone by then and he would make sure that his new wife was with him, too. Rolling the small cart, its utensils and lids drumming slightly against silver edges like a heartbeat, his heart melted as he saw his wife sit up in the four-poster bed.

"I'm so hungry," she said.

Omar sat on the side of the bed and watched Pilar begin to eat. Together they ate in silence until his wife started to talk about her crazy plans again.

"Baltimore is between New York and Washington," Pilar said. "One of the girls at the club found out from a tourist."

"What if I don't want to go?"

"You'll go."

"What if I want to stay here and be with my wife? What if I told you that they've decided to take Carmelo instead?"

Carmelo had been his best man, too. All thumbs, he barely held onto the rings during the ceremony. Omar knew that Pilar so disliked him.

"No, you wouldn't," she said.

"Why not?"

"Remember our plan."

Omar hushed her and nodded at the ceiling. "Please, my angel," he warned, "you're never sure who's listening."

But that only made her angry, more defiant.

"Why would they eavesdrop on us?"

Omar shrugged.

"To hear the greatest third baseman in Cuba talk to his bride?" she said, her voice rising. "You're telling me that they are that demented?"

They ate in silence until Omar tried again.

"Listen, darling, I really don't have to go to Baltimore," he told her. "Carmelo can take my place if I want it. I'm not spoiling to play those Orioles again. There will be other times, the next Olympics. There's talk of a home-and-away series against the Americans every spring."

"Omar, you need to go now," she said. "Don't talk to me of other chances."

He whistled softly, trying to laugh. "My angel, how you think sometimes. Pilar, if I got away, for real, it could be a long time before we see each other again. My God, if I did such a thing they would make life miserable for you here."

"I would survive it," she snapped.

"Pilar," Omar said as he watched her take the last edge of white toast into her mouth. He picked up a silver fork, ready for more, but there wasn't any food remaining.

"It is our morning to remember," he said, putting the fork back down. He reached over to stroke her bare shoulder, but Pilar was already up, the sheet still wrapped around her, striding out to the balcony.

Omar followed and together they stood there in the morning sun and watched the biplane bank and begin to return back to Havana.

"Fool," Pilar hissed and at first Omar feared that she was speaking about him. But then he saw that her eyes were on the plane and its lazy trajectory back toward the island.

"When I was little, Grandpa used to tell me about how the casinos and the old hotels—the Capri, the Nacional—were open at all hours. How Cuba was a carnival and everybody beat a path to our door."

She stopped a moment to look at him and then back out at the approaching plane before continuing.

"There was as much corruption and wickedness then as there is now. But instead of being nothing, absolutely nothing, Cuba was where they dreamed of coming. Can you believe it, Omar? Grandpa said that early every morning the night ferry from Miami would dock and the Cadillacs, Studebakers, and Hudsons would come off the ramp—everybody so happy to be here and in a hurry to see it all."

Omar went to put his arm over her shoulder, to pull her close, but Pilar shrugged him off.

"That's why the one on that plane is so stupid," she said. "If I was at the controls, I'd keep going, no matter how many fighter planes Fidel called into the sky."

THREE

O N SATURDAY AFTERNOON, when the last busload of Germans or Canadians or Venezuelans left to go home, that's when they divided up the loot at Cayo Coco. Luz loved that word—*loot*. It was something nobody in Cuba had said until a few years ago. Pilar had been the first one to speak it in their circles, and Luz especially liked how the word sat in her head, like a sweet lie. *Loot*. It was all that life often was, and the key was how it was divided up.

Pilar hadn't arrived yet. She and Luz were there to represent the forty dancers that worked at the resort. The second-highest number at any resort on the island—behind only the famed Tropicana back in Havana. Some of the other regulars were missing, too, but that didn't stop Livan from wanting to start right in.

"Let's get this done," he said as he sat down at the green plastic table in the shade by the pool. He pushed two bottles of Finesse shampoo and a pair of tweezers into the small pile of toiletries and various other odds and ends that made up this week's take.

Also on the table were two bars of Irish Spring with aloe, three boxes of Kleenex, a Mach3 razor, a Revlon lipstick in muted pink, an orange can of Edge Protective Shave and a paperback book in English, as well as three T-shirts and two pairs of Teva sandals. Whatever was left behind by the tourists at Cayo Coco during the previous week was brought here, to the Loot Party, to be divvied up early Saturday afternoons before the next load of tourists arrived from the Jose Marti International Airport.

Luz couldn't take her eyes off the lipstick in muted pink. That was the real find in this mess, and Pilar would certainly think the same. Where was Pilar anyway? It wasn't like her to be late for the weekly Loot Party.

"They didn't leave us much," said Elena, the resort's head maid.

"When do they?" Livan complained.

Beside him, Jorge only nodded in agreement with what his comic partner said. Even off stage, anyone could tell that Livan, the taller of the two, was the impetuous one, the guy who came up with the best jokes, like the recent classic about the Russians. On and off the stage, Jorge was content to play the straight man.

"You remember those Americans," Jorge began, the words just tumbling out. "They only left with the clothes on their backs. Everything else was for us."

"How can we forget them?" Livan interrupted. "When that's all you talk about—the Americans, the Americans."

"I still don't know how they came here," Elena said, flashing a mouth of misaligned yellow teeth.

"The Americans," Luz repeated and it came out almost as a prayer, and Elena and Jorge nodded in agreement.

"Enough," Livan snapped. "Let's finish this. I have too much to do before the next group comes in."

Pablo, the kid who tended to the boats and equipment at the beach, only now arrived. He's more deferential than Jorge, Luz thought, as she watched him sit down at the plastic table, as far away from Livan as he could be. Pablo didn't make eye contact with anybody, but he did mumble, "Pilar's coming."

How would he know that? Luz wondered.

"I'm not waiting anymore," Livan said. "Jorge and I want the razor and cream." He reached for those items. "The rest of you can divide up the rest."

"But what about Pablo?"

It was Pilar, dressed in cut-off jeans that accented her legs and a button-down shirt courtesy of a previous Loot Party. Luz couldn't help but smile as her best friend slid into the remaining chair next to her and the men's eyes momentarily locked upon her beauty.

"What about Pablo?" Livan replied.

"He should get one of them, if he wants."

"He can have the soap. He sure needs it."

The last comment set everyone to scolding Livan and he tried to laugh it off. Sometimes Livan reminded Luz of Carmelo, the best man at Pilar's wedding. Both thought that nothing could touch them. That they could say the most terrible things to other people and then just shrug it off.

"The soap is fine," Pablo said. "I'll share it with Edmundo."

Edmundo was the head lifeguard down at the beach, slightly younger than Pablo.

Pablo's talk of sharing briefly quieted everybody. Perhaps it appealed to the talk of socialism that Fidel and the elders had ladled on thick over the years. Whatever the reason, from then on the Loot Party moved ahead with more common courtesy and respect. The shaving cream and razor did go to Livan and Jorge. The soap to Pablo. The T-shirts and sandals were passed around the table and eventually went to Jorge and Elena. With clothes, it was easier to simply let things be decided by fit. It was fairer and in a strange way allowed everyone to look ahead to the future. If something didn't fit this week, perhaps next week it would.

Piece by piece, the loot was handed out until only the lipstick and the book were left.

"I'd like the lipstick," Luz said and everyone grew quiet, seeing if anybody would contest the request.

"I like it, too," Elena said.

Luz nodded. "Okay, we'll both try it."

She held the golden cylinder out to the older woman, who was the head of the cleaning crew. Elena's hands trembled slightly as she delicately took off the cap and turned the end until the first hint of lipstick appeared. With a faint smile, Elena applied a thin coat to the lower and then the upper lip.

Elena smoothed her lips together and smiled. Luz thought she looked ridiculous, like a clown really, but everybody, even Livan, knew enough to coo and nod in approval. For a moment, Luz feared that the old woman would be awarded the lipstick simply out of charity. And Pilar must have sensed the same thing, for she held out her hand for the lipstick. Elena reluctantly passed the cylinder to her, and they watched as Pilar expertly applied it.

"Luz and I would share this," she murmured.

Pilar sat there and turned her pretty head from one side to the other, so everyone could see. Luz saw how a dreamy look fell into the eyes of the men and Pablo. What any of them would give to kiss her best friend right here and now.

Livan was the first to break out of the spell.

"It's yours," he said and nodded to Pilar and Luz, and nobody argued.

The only thing left on the table was the paperback book by Jack Kerouac. For a moment, everybody considered it, not sure what to do. Finally, Livan picked it up and flipped once through the pages.

"It's too much in English. I cannot read this," he said. "I know you can, beach boy. I hear you have the tongue."

With that, he flipped the book to Pablo, and another Loot Party had ended.

FOUR

JAIME WAS CRYING IN THE PARLOR and Maria wondered if she should go down and comfort him. It was about the car again. She just knew it. She told him to keep that car to himself. Not to take others around in it, no matter how good the money may be. But Maria realized that he really doesn't listen to her anymore. She wondered how much he ever did.

When she went downstairs, he was pacing the length of the living room—the television was turned up loud and Fidel was addressing the nation, again. Musicians from around the world had come to Cuba. For the next few days they would be composing music together. International recording stars matched up with Cuban acts. "That is how we can be in this world," Fidel told the national television audience. "At one with the music that rings through it."

Jaime was paying no attention to *El Jefe*. Her husband's face had become all twisted and flush, but she knew she couldn't comment about the crying. At least not to his face. That would be too much for him. To admit to such a thing. A middle-aged man crying. That simply isn't done.

"What happened?" Maria asked and sat down on the couch, watching him, wary to see if he lashed out again. Goes to hit the wall or the tabletop. How long before he strikes her?

Everybody, even his brother Luis, had to agree that things hadn't been easy since Jaime had lost his job with United Press International. It was if Jaime had become tainted somehow. That taking the foreigners' money meant that he couldn't be trusted anymore. This, of course, was so much nonsense. Jaime remained as true as the summer sun in the morning sky. In her heart, Maria had known that since the first day she saw him, more than twenty-five years ago.

Two people don't raise a child as willful as Pilar and keep a roof over their heads, despite everything that has happened to this country, without some feeling always being there. Still, there were times when Maria wondered if love can be so strong, so constant, that it can be forgotten. Strange, wasn't it? But she realized that both of them do it: Count on the other so much, they never say a word about the ties that bind everything else together. They just know and believe that the other one will always be there. But if you don't acknowledge such things, well, that's when the bad feelings can build up. And before you know it, you're both on the opposite ends of everything, looking across at the other, wondering how you could be so stupid to marry this one, a person you seem to have nothing in common with anymore.

"Damn fools," Jaime said. He spat out the words like they were poison. "They had no right to do it."

"What did they do, my darling?"

"Stop me. I had done nothing wrong."

"Except have foreigners in your car."

"Now you," he glared at Maria. "Now you are sounding like them."

"You know that's not true," she replied, quieter now, praying he will see that she was on his side. "But you know how they are. They see a Cuban with a foreigner and immediately there's going to be questions. Where did it happen?"

"In front of the Hotel Inglaterra."

"You pulled up in front?"

"Yes, so I am an idiot. I wasn't thinking. My dear, I don't know what it is. Sometimes when I'm with those people and I hear them talk about their lives and they are speaking with me, just telling me things like I was their best friend. Oh, dear God, it's like I've fallen into their world. I grow dumb with it all. I forget to do things correctly. They offer to buy my dinner at the Club Rio or the Nacional. And, yes, I do break bread with them. And I feel like I could be one of them. You know, in another time, another place."

"Who stopped you?"

"The hotel security. They had been keeping track of me since yesterday. Sometimes I'm so stupid. They brought over the street police. They gave me this."

He pulled a crumbled piece of paper from his pocket and held it out to her. Maria reluctantly took it from him and suddenly he was on his knees in front of her, his head in her lap, crying tears he didn't want anyone to see.

The citation called for her Jaime to obtain a license for driving tourists. Cost: Three hundred dollars. If he didn't get the license, if he was ever stopped again, he could lose his car.

Even Maria admitted that his car is a beauty. A '94 Honda Civic. It was the office car for UPI. When they pulled out, the car was left to him. After all, he had been a loyal employee—more than willing to drive to anywhere whenever anybody asked. She remembered the times she criticized him for being that way. Told him they would never remember such kindness. But she was wrong. When they closed their bureau, Jaime got the car. It was easier than trying to take the vehicle off the island.

On Sunday afternoons, Jaime could be found in the driveway, stooped under the mango tree, washing that car's silver skin until it shone in the sun. The neighbors teased Maria about how he loves that car. That he loves it more than he does his wife. But Maria only smiled and told herself that it isn't true.

"So you just won't drive tourists anymore," she said. "It's that simple."

Jaime looked up at her as if she had asked him to give up one of the things he loves most in the world. Jaime remained silent for a long time and then said, "I can find three hundred dollars."

"Darling, don't be crazy," Maria said. "Even if we had three hundred dollars, we have so many other wants. The washer is going. And what about the roof?"

"These ones I was driving today," he continued. "Two Americans, can you believe it? They felt bad for me. They tipped me an extra one hundred, so I only need two hundred. Then I could get the license. I'd be legal then."

"But, Jaime, you know how it works," his wife said and stroked the top of his head. His soft thick hair was becoming flecked with gray. "It won't be just three hundred. There will be the other bribes once you go down to the station. It isn't so easy to be legal."

"I know, I know."

"Why drive them? Keep your car in the garage. Let it rest."

There was a knock at the door. Jaime struggled to his feet, wiping the tears away with the back of his hand.

"Don't worry," Maria said. "I'll see who it is."

She opened the door only a crack, peering out, until she saw the smiling pie face of Luis, Jaime's baby brother.

"You," she said and opened the door wide.

The two brothers were rarely the best of friends. But his arrival, especially now, was a blessing. A rainbow amid the tears.

"What's the occasion?" she asked as he stepped inside.

"I have more pictures from the wedding," Luis said in that fast-paced voice of his. "You remember, Maria. I had to send them to Mexico for processing. I wanted them done on that special glossy paper."

He held out the envelope to her. "Our Pilar," Luis added. "What a lovely bride."

"Yes, she was," Maria said and took the envelope from her brother-in-law. But marriage, even to a catch like Omar, hadn't truly satisfied her only child. No, Pilar still talked about wanting to go to America. Why couldn't she ever be satisfied with what she had?

Maria sat down on the couch and the two brothers fell in on either side of her. They were so different. Her Jamie was tall and quiet, with his dark moods, while Luis bounded into everything like a cuddly dog. She couldn't remember the last time she saw him sad, at a loss about the state of things, no matter how bad things can be in this special period in time of peace.

As the brothers watched her, Maria spread the photos out on the small lacquered table in the parlor. She glanced back at her husband. Only a few moments before, with Luis at the door, Jaime had disappeared into the kitchen to wipe his hands on a dish rag. How quickly he could cover everything up, Maria thought. The skin around his eyes was barely red.

Everybody leaned in closer to study the glowing images of Pilar in her wedding gown on the veranda at the Habana Libre. She, Omar, the best man Carmelo stood together, smiling like starlets from of an old Hollywood movie.

"So nice," Jaime said and turned to find his brother smiling at him. At such moments it seemed like Luis was only put on earth to make them happy. "Thank you."

"The pleasure is all mine," Luis answered as Maria slowly flipped through each photo in the set of sixty-four, carefully laying them down one atop the other when she was done. Pilar was in almost every one, as well she should have been. It was her special day.

"So, what are you two lovebirds up to?" Luis asked as Maria lingered on the final shot—one of Pilar flanked by her and Jaime. God, she was a beautiful child. The same high proud forehead as Maria's grandfather and the sharp angles and cheekbones of Jaime's side of the family. The smile that was so infectious—part devil, part angel. In a perfect world, Maria would have had many more like her.

Maria glanced back at Jaime before saying, "Luis, I was trying to convince my husband to give me a ride in his beautiful car."

"A ride?" Luis said. "Where are we going?"

"Anywhere," Maria said.

"But Industralies is playing Pinar del Rio on television," Jaime protested.

"How can we watch another game after that one last week," Maria said. "Isn't that right, Luis? You were there, right?"

"What a game it was," Luis said. "Our Team Cuba should have won. They outplayed those Orioles from Baltimore. Anyone could see it. Omar was our star."

"If he had gotten a hit in the eleventh inning," Jaime said, "they would have won."

"Don't be like that," Maria said.

"I'm not criticizing him. But that's the truth."

Sensing trouble, Luis broke in. "The main thing is we proved we can play with them. Anybody could see that Cuba should have won. And Omar was marvelous to watch. When he plays up in Baltimore, more people will see how good he truly is."

For a long moment, the three of them considered how the great Omar Silva, the best third baseman that Cuba had ever produced, could slip away from the team when it visited the United States. How he could do it and nobody would blame him. Not even his new bride, their Pilar.

"And the musicians are still at the Hotel Nacional," Luis said, once again the one trying to smooth things over.

"And you've been there, too?" his older brother asked. "I don't believe it."

"Yes," Luis said sheepishly. "I found that I couldn't stay away."

"We'll include it in on our grand tour of the city," Maria said.

Her husband still had a puzzled look on his face, but Luis, he got it. He was already standing up, ready to go.

"Can I come, too?" he asked.

"Of course, you can come," Maria said. "We'll all go. It will be like the old days."

She pulled Jaime by one hand toward the front door.

"Right now I want to pretend that I'm a rich tourist who wants to see all of Havana," she said to her husband of almost twenty-five years. "Come, you'll take me."

Outside they found the silver Honda. The pride of Jaime's life. Luis had had the courtesy to park his blue Audi, a newer car actually, out on the street. Fearful that things would unravel, that her husband would become stubborn again, Maria hurried to the Honda's passenger side and opened the door. Luis slid into the back seat, and Jaime had little choice but to go around to the driver's side. Before he could say another word, Maria had settled into the passenger seat. Ready to ride shotgun. *Shotgun.* That was another strange word the foreign visitors had taught her husband.

"My Maria," he said once they are all inside. "This is crazy."

"I don't care, Jaime. It's been so long since I've seen the city at night. Please drive me along the Malecon. That's all I ask. Pretend that I'm a rich one, too."

"But it isn't the money," he said. "It's how they talk. How they are with the world."

Jaime sat with two hands on the steering wheel, staring out of the windshield, up into the sky somewhere.

"They know so much," he said. "The words just roll off their tongues. They know about what is happening not only America, but in Europe, too. Listening to them is like falling into some wide, fast river. It rides up underneath you and carries you away."

"You must enjoy their company more than mine."

"I didn't say that."

"Well, then prove it. Drive me."

"Drive us," chimed in his little brother from the backseat.

Shaking his head, Jaime started up the engine and carefully backed out of the short driveway and on to the street. It was going on nine at night and there were few other vehicles out. They went down Castelle Calle and past the park, angling for the sea.

Soon enough they roared by the glowing entrances to the tunnels—the places that were designed to save everyone if the Americans ever invaded. Maria recognized the one up ahead. It was where she and Jaime first made love. Getting into the spirit of things, Jaime briefly tooted the horn as they sped past, and Maria and him exchanged glances, remembering when their only goal in life was to find a place to lay together. Having to go to other people's apartments—desperate for any privacy. What joy when Jaime was assigned to guard duty and given keys to the tunnels that pocketed the hills of the old city.

She remembered the silence of those places. The rows and rows of medical supplies and the squeaky military beds. Only in case of invasion were the tunnels to be opened. Maintaining them was one of Fidel's top priorities. And seeing the Americans never did mount a real attack, or at least didn't try again after the Bay of Pigs, it made one wonder if word hadn't filtered out. That the world, on some high level, knew that the Cuban people would never be overwhelmed again. That they were ready to repel all intruders.

She knew that Jaime pointed out the tunnels to the foreigners when they rode in his car. The city and the surrounding the country-side were honeycombed with them. But they remained an illusion. Only seen when somebody else, a Cuban who lived here, acknowledged them. The rest of Cuba could go to waste, but the people would always be ready to fight. When the day of reckoning came, the tunnels could still open and shelter enough until the new dawn arrived.

Maria recalled what her father used to say, "We Cubans have learned to live without the bad and without the good."

Down along the Malecon, she saw that kids had built small fires on the sea wall. Some had guitars and Maria heard their singing as they rolled past, going all the way to El Morro Castle. Until a few years ago, this was where Pilar could be found. At first, Maria thought her daughter was simply caught up in the singing, being around the other teenagers. But then she heard the stories about how Pilar had the courage to chat up the tourists. Did so, even though some probably got the wrong idea about her advances. Her daughter was like her husband—too curious about what went on beyond these shores. Maria had hoped that getting married, especially to somebody like Omar, would end all that. But the other afternoon, Elena, the head maid from Cayo Coco had stopped by. Maria had known Elena since grammar school.

"It's the most curious thing," Elena told Maria over tea. "Pilar and her friend Luz were given this stick of lipstick, the most beautiful shade of pink, at one of our weekly meetings. It was something a tourist had left behind. I was interested it, too, but I didn't think anymore about it after the others decided. The next day Pilar finds me and just gives it away to me. But then she asks if I can sneak her into a guest room every now and then. Maria, your daughter loves to watch these shows—MTV, HBO, even CNN Headline News."

Maria tried her best to put on a brave face for her old friend. She told Elena it was nothing. But afterward, as she was cooking dinner, her eyes welled with tears. Since Pilar had been a small girl she had been infatuated with worlds she had no business being in.

"So many *jineteras*," Luis yelled out from the back seat.

Packs of young girls in spandex and high heels moved out from the shadows when they saw Jaime's polished car.

"They know about the musicians in town, at the Nacional," Luis continued in an excited voice. "They'd like nothing better than to bed one of them."

Her husband accelerated away from the prostitutes. The wind felt good in her hair and Maria understood why Jaime enjoyed such times.

"Tell me what you tell them," she said.

"What," he asks over the roar of the breeze coming through the open windows.

"If I was a tourist, what would you be telling me now?"

"Maria, stop."

"Tell her," Luis shouted out from the back seat. "Tell me."

"I would tell them about the castle," Jaime began. "How it is the oldest in the Caribbean. How once Havana was the center of shipping and so much of the treasure found in the New World came here before being sent on to Spain. How we Cubans are proud of that. How we will never forget it."

"Do you tell them about your famous son-in-law?" Luis said. "Omar Silva, the best ballplayer on the national team."

"No, not yet," Jaime said, keeping his eyes on the wide boulevard that kissed the edge of Old Havana and then ran along the deep-water harbor.

"But you will," Maria smiled. The wind has made a mess of her long black hair with its multiplying strands of gray. But she didn't mind. Not tonight.

"And he should," Luis called out from the back seat. "I heard that he hit two homeruns in training with a wooden bat. That's what they're making them use to play the major leaguers up in Baltimore. No aluminum bats."

When they returned home, Jaime carefully pulled the Honda into the garage. Luis said goodnight after Maria invited him over for Sunday dinner. She had found flour and watercress at the Dollar Store. It would be the most anticipated meal since Pilar and Omar's wedding.

Once the house became quiet and dark, she found Jaime in the parlor, holding the photos of their lovely daughter up to the light.

"Come," she says and took him by the hand.

Upstairs they made love almost as well as they did years ago in the tunnels.

"Let me see if I can get the license," he said in a dreamy voice before nodding off.

When Maria didn't object, her husband took such hesitation for approval.

As he began to snore, she walked about the room, thinking about what three hundred dollars would mean to the family. Such a sum would stabilize them in this crazy era, this special time in the period of peace, as Fidel, the crazy uncle who still ran this nation, called it. My god, three hundred dollars.

Maria lay back down, next to her husband, running her hand softly across his chest. He groaned softly and rolled over on his side.

She could try and stop her husband, but would it be worth the aggravation?

A half-moon hung in the sky and she reached underneath the bed and pulled out a small wooden box. Inside were the baby teeth from Pilar's childhood. The foreigners told Jaime about this magical being that gives money to children when they lose their teeth. A fairy prince who steals into their rooms and with a sleight of hand takes the tooth from underneath a pillow and leaves a coin, even a dollar bill, in its place. Pilar always loved that story.

Maria couldn't see throwing her child's teeth away, even for an American fairy tale, so she kept them here—in a small wooden box that Luis bought for her years ago when he went to Mexico on business. Not even Jaime knew she had these baby teeth. It was almost embarrassing how sentimental she could be sometimes.

In the moonlight, with her husband, who sometimes made no sense, Maria let her fingertips run across the smooth enamel. She felt the sharp edges as her hand trailed back and forth across the small bits as if she was playing some strange instrument. Only then did the world slow down for her. Only then did she find the peace that would allow her to fall asleep.

FIVE

H ERE SHE CAME AGAIN, down the boardwalk, seeking him
out. Pablo had overheard that word—*boardwalk*—only a few
weeks ago from some Canadian tourists. "Look, honey, it's a boardwalk like in Jersey."

Pablo had no idea where Jersey was or exactly what a boardwalk
was. But he liked the sound of both words. In between the afternoon
and evening shows, the showgirl had routinely gone in search of him
and once again there was nothing Pablo could do to avoid her.

He was putting away the boats and jet skis for the day. She paused
on the rail of the boardwalk and looked down at him. Then her gaze
shifted to take in the Hobie Cat, the newest boat in the fleet—the one
with the tallest mast and the largest sail. Its sleek twin hulls were
light green.

"How long is the passage in that?" she asked.

Thankfully, there was nobody else at the lagoon. But Pablo act-
ed like there was. He dipped the plastic bucket into the water and
doused another section of the wooden deck. Everything had to be
cleaned up and put away at nightfall.

"Pablo, you heard me," she repeated.

The boy dunked the bucket into the warm water again and then
let it rest on the deck.

"It depends on the wind," he said. "I've already told you that, Pilar."

"How about on a day like today?"

Impatiently, he flung another bucketful across the glistening canvas deck and then sprayed off the soap and saltwater with the hose.
He paused and gazed out to the ocean, out past the surf line.

"Two, maybe three days," he said and returned to his chores.

"You should try again," Pilar said.

Pablo gazed up at her. The steady breeze was making a mess of her long black hair. She kept smoothing it behind one ear, but all that did was reveal more of her face—the full lips that fell naturally into a pout, the regal Spanish nose, the dark eyes that took in his every move.

"I told you," he hissed. "I'm never trying again."

"There's no reason to be afraid," she said. "Not around me."

Pilar stepped closer, leaning over the rail on tip-toe, the angle revealing her ample cleavage, her ass rising as if she was about to be taken by one of the male tourists. For that had been the whispers about Pilar before her recent marriage. How she had a sweet tooth for the barracudas that would pay for a Cuban beauty to show them the seedier side of the capital, Havana. She was their girl.

"Your husband's going to *El Norte* soon," Pablo said. "I heard it on the radio."

He was pleased with himself as the glimmer of what he took to be concern, maybe anger, flashed across her face. There, that had stopped her, but only for a moment.

"Yes he does," she replied. "To play the Orioles again."

How quickly she regained her composure. Pablo could almost imagine her being back up on stage, front and center at the Cayo Coco. Her arms outstretched. Her glorious body dappled with the glints of white light reflecting off the silver disco ball that they lowered from the high ceiling for the last song of the night, Gloria Gaynor's "I Will Survive."

He'd seen how she and the other dancers had finished their final routine and then had to stand there, the light breaking up around them, as the crowd rose into a standing ovation. It was always Pilar in the center and her best friend, Luz, on her right. They were like statues, caught in freeze frame, somehow holding it together, until the final curtain went down.

"My husband is my concern," Pilar said. "But, remember, the next time you try, you talk to me beforehand."

"Pilar, I told you—"

"You'll try again and you'll try again soon. If not maybe somebody goes to talk to Asafa. Imagine what the boss man would do if he knew the truth about the other night?"

"You wouldn't."

"Pablo, don't tease a tease."

"Pilar, please, no more of this crazy talk. I'm not trying again. You have my word on that."

"No, you'll try again," she said. "I can see it in your eyes. You almost slipped away from here and you won't forget that. I know I couldn't forget it."

"It's not what you think," Pablo protested.

As they spoke, he coiled the last of the ropes on the wooden docks. He coiled them in perfect circles. But when it came to do the last one, his fingertips began to shake. He tried several times before throwing the loose rope onto the deck, disgusted with himself.

"Leave me alone," he begged.

"I cannot do that," she replied, still leaning over from the rail. She hovered above him like a misguided angel as he knelt on the dock below. "When you go, I will go with you. I'm thinking perhaps we should go soon."

***

A few nights later, before the dinner show, Pilar and Luz stood side by side, putting on their makeup. They were already dressed in their rhinestone briefs, golden-colored bra cups, and heels. The only things remaining were the makeup and headdresses. For the evening show, they always wore the ones with the flush plumage, the ones with the ostrich feathers.

"You'll have to find another way to the Tropicana tonight," Pilar said. She then brought her lips together into a kiss to check the lipstick coverage.

"You're not going?" Luz replied.

Neither of them looked away from their reflection in the wall mirror. Pilar began to comb out her long hair, while Luz worked on her lashes with dark eyeliner.

"I'm too tired," Pilar said and Luz didn't answer right away. For as long as she could remember Thursday night had been their time to go to the Trop, their old stomping grounds, where they used to turn an odd trick in the parking lot. Sometimes Luz still did. She was sure Pilar had moved past those days. After all, her best friend was married now, to a famous ballplayer to boot.

"You wouldn't be so tired, if you weren't always walking down to the beach," Luz said. Then she quickly added, eager to change the subject, "Where'd that new lipstick go?"

"I gave it to Elena," Pilar said.

"Elena," Luz replied and looked at her friend for the first time instead of stealing glances at her reflection in the dressing room mirror.

"She looked good in it. I felt sorry for her."

Luz snorted dismissively. "The last time Elena looked good in lipstick was when Fidel was a pup and you know it."

When Pilar didn't reply, Luz's talk became braver.

"And as for you, darling, if you keep going down to the beach, you'll get too dark. Men don't like Spanish woman who are too dark. You know that. God knows you talk to that beach boy so much. That—"

"Pablo."

"That's right. He's your new best friend. How is he wearing you out?"

"Stop it," Pilar snapped and Luz looked chastened for a moment or two.

"I'm just tired," Pilar continued. "That's all. Omar's been in Pinar del Rio with the team, training. They leave for Baltimore tomorrow. He won't be home before the flight to the United States. I just want to go to bed early for a change."

Luz finished with the eyeliner and briefly considered her reflection in the mirror. She was good-looking. She knew that. But she also knew she would never be as good-looking as Pilar.

"You're not pregnant, are you?" Luz blurted out.

"No."

"I'm serious. That's what my mother says. A woman gets married and then comes the child. No matter how a girl may plan otherwise, that's the way it goes."

The door to the dressing room opened and one of the stagehands shouted, "Three minutes to curtain."

Pilar put down the brush and the two friends helped each other put on the heavy headdresses.

"Am I straight?" Luz asked.

"Perfect," Pilar replied and turned for the stage door.

***

As soon as the klieg lights hit them—the smaller spots from both sides and the major blast of brightness coming at them right in the middle of the room, just above eye level—Pilar had her arms extended at right angles. With higher and higher leg kicks she led them out onto the cream-colored stage, until they were at the lip of the orchestra pit and the crowd was rising to its feet to whistle and cheer. Luz fell into her regular spot, just alongside her best friend, and for the first few minutes, as the band played a sexier, raunchier version of a French cancan, she and the other girls struggled to keep up with Pilar, their leader. Tonight Pilar seemed determined on driving them to the brink of exhaustion. The last kicks were as high as any of them could go and now Pilar switched to an extravagant bump and grind, the arms still extended, head straight and smile beaming. If Luz had had the chance she would have asked her friend why they were going so fast, so hard; after all, it was their second show of the day. Usually they coasted a bit for the late evening show. The crowd was undoubtedly drunker than earlier in the day. Nobody really cared how much they actually danced as long as a long shank of leg and plenty of cleavage was visible. And such things were always visible at Cayo Coco. But Pilar was having none of it. Tonight she danced like a crazy person and the rest of the group had no choice but to race to keep up. For the full ten minutes, Pilar kept up the pace until they were finally backstage breathless, beads of perspiration matting down their hair under the headdresses and rivulets slipping down their spines.

"I thought you were tired?" Luz admonished Pilar as they filed back to the dressing room. "What are you doing pushing us like that?"

But Pilar ignored her. She just gazed back at Luz with a smile of rapture and contentment. She looked so happy Luz didn't know what to say next, so they again fell into silence as they concentrated on their reflections in the dressing room mirror. Off came the makeup that had been painstakingly put on only minutes before.

A knock on the door brought forth a bouquet of pink roses. One of the stagehands made the delivery. They were for Luz, from a trim barracuda in a dark silk shirt, freshly creased pants and Italian shoes, who nodded from the shadows outside.

"What do you think?" Luz said before she took another long in-hale of the roses' sweet scent.

She later remembered how Pilar glanced at the man's image in the mirror and then asked, "Where's he from?"

"Somewhere in Canada," Luz had answered. Already she had the heavy makeup off. Only a hint of eyeliner and lipstick left. "Some-place called Ottawa."

"Go," Pilar said. "Have fun."

It wasn't until days later that Luz remembered those words and realized how unusual they were. How so unlike Pilar. Wasn't Pilar the one who warned her to go slow, not to fuck so soon? Let them spend some money on you first. At least buy you a good meal before it all began again. But on this night she had said none of those things.

SIX

HOW SOON THEIR WORLD FELL AWAY FROM THEM. The twin silver towers of the Cayo Coco that flank the egg-shaped ballroom, where Pablo had stolen in to see Pilar dance, faded from view much faster than he expected. Too soon the country became a long, cigar-stretch of land with only a smattering of lights. For as long as Pablo could remember, he had been told that the Americans would invade someday. That they were intent on transforming the island into another Puerto Rico, or what they've done with huge portions of Mexico. His grandfather, who had sold trinkets and home-made dolls out of ribbons of scrap cloth, once told him such things. His grandfather made it sound as if the Americans would never succeed. How Cuba was such a strong nation. That it would unite, as one, and fight on into the night.

But as Pablo and Pilar sailed silently away from Cayo Coco aboard the Hobie Cat that night after the late show, away from everything they had ever known, the boy couldn't help thinking that it would have been so easy for the Yanquis, and anybody else with gunboats and armed men and evil intent, to sweep in on a night like this and simply take over. Clouds veiled much of the stars and any brightness from the half-moon faded in and out, nothing more than a rumor really, as it rose into a threatening sky.

Perhaps we have survived this long, Pablo thought, the tiller stick resting in his hand, because the rest of the world has forgotten about us. He had friends who sneaked into tourists' rooms to watch CNN and the television channels from *El Norte*. Rumor had it that his traveling companion often made deals with Elena, the head of the cleaning crew, to watch the forbidden American channels. But no matter. Pablo's friends told him it was all about the Middle East now: Iraq, Iran, Israel, and other countries that he had a difficult time holding in his head.

Pilar was scared. He could tell, but she'd be damned if she would say anything about it. So beautiful, so proud. As soon as they had shoved off from the beach, a few minutes before midnight, she had grown quiet about what they were doing. What they had done to put this into motion.

Pilar had come down to the boats still flush from the night's last show. If Pablo had been a stronger man, an older one, he would have told her to go away. Don't bother me. That they weren't going anywhere tonight. No matter what had been discussed. Maybe they could have lingered again in the shadows under the Jersey boardwalk and perhaps he could have kissed her and hushed her, told her to be still, as he ran his fingers up her long leg. She didn't give him much. Still, Pablo, in recent weeks, had become more determined. He was beginning to learn that men don't wait for a perfect chance. They just plunge ahead. Boys wait and wait and wait.

Besides that was part of their deal—he and Pilar's. It was never spoken, put out there on the table like the weekly Loot Party, with everyone chiming in. Still, if she wanted to come along when he sailed, part of the deal was that he could kiss her lips at the end of another night of argument and planning. Her lips were like an exotic fruit. Firm like a mango, but smelling of powder and aglow with rouge in the night light.

When she kissed him that first time, almost taking pity on him, Pablo felt everything rise right up through his head until he nearly fainted. He remembered that Pilar had laughed. She was an inch or two taller than him, even without heels.

Sliding her hand deftly down the front of his T-shirt, now inside the white Cayo Coco shorts, she had him out, holding it in her hand, so fast he wasn't sure what was happening. There she paused, smiled at him, and then sank to one knee and took him in her mouth. It was over in a heartbeat or two. Pilar had obviously done this before.

She briefly laughed as he zipped himself back up.

"When you go," she said, "I'm with you."

Pablo nodded, lost in the profound happiness he felt.

But tonight, as they moved rapidly away from the shore, the sails filling with the freshening breeze, he wished that his Pilar would be as sure of herself now as she was during those nights of preparation. When she let him stroke her leg, touch her fingertips, even once kiss her breasts. It made Pablo nervous that she had grown so quiet.

Looking back at the fading shoreline, only a few lights visible now, he tried to steer them in a northeasterly direction. He had lashed the compass that she found for them on the stern end of the canvas that straddled both hulls. The night sky was overcast, which was good, what they had planned for. For a moment, though, Pablo longed to gaze up at the stars and try to recite every constellation he could remember.

They had to be five miles out by now—technically safe in international waters. Still, if one of Fidel's gunboats saw them, it would show no reluctance in towing them back into port. A part of Pablo wouldn't mind such a scene. The look on Asafa's face would last a lifetime. To prove to him that his beach boy, the one he loved to boss around so much, had *cojones*, too. But in the next breath, Pablo told himself that it was far better if he never came across that man or his like again.

Far off to our left, two freighters made the long left-hand turn into the narrow channel for Havana, the oldest port in the New World. Atop the bluff nearer to them, he could make out the flashing white light for El Morro Castle. How had it come to this? At one point in time, Cuba was a respected land. The place where everything of worth, all the gold and silver found by the conquistadors, flowed through before being sent on to mother Spain. Now nothing of consequence came into the country anymore. Back at Cayo Coco, they talked about the American musicians who were at the Hotel Nacional. What a tremendous feat that was. But that was just politics talking. Always politics and Fidel.

***

In a few hours, the sun rose bloody and bright, and Pablo could feel his heart sink. He didn't dare tell her the old sailor's superstition: "Red sky in morning, sailor take warning." It was better that she didn't know any of that.

"Come here," Pablo told her. "Your turn to steer."

"But I don't know anything about that," Pilar replied.

"Then you need to learn," Pablo said, trying to keep his voice low and serious, making it sound more like a man's voice.

Reluctantly, Pilar slid across the canvas that stretched from one fiberglass hull to the other, all the way to the back end of the Hobie.

"You need breakfast," she said, holding up an orange. Pablo took it from her, almost wondering if this would be another one of her tricks. Another tease.

"I'll teach you about the boat," he said.

"Why?" she asked, digging through the small chest of foodstuffs and pulling out another orange. She tore into its tender skin with her teeth and then dug deep with her polished fingernails.

"Because I cannot do it all by myself."

She seemed to agree with this and slid closer to Pablo. She stretched her long dancer legs out in front of her. Her family laid claim to have descended from the top families in Spain centuries ago. Pablo had seen her Uncle Luis at the club and heard him carry on, like he once sat on the right hand of the king himself. But Pablo noticed he had thinner ankles than Pilar. Those legs of hers may be a dream, but they lead up to the beginnings of a generous ass. In the morning light, her light skin showed that it could grow as dark as his if she was out in the sun more. Somewhere along the family line, an African or two must have jumped the fence, as Pablo's grandfather used to say. In Cuba, nobody could really claim to be above anybody else. That's maybe the only thing the party and Fidel talked about that Pablo totally agreed with. We're all in this together.

"This is the tiller," he told Pilar.

She screwed her face up in contempt. They had gone out twice before, in the dark, after she was finished dancing for the night. That was their only real practice aboard the boat.

"Remember it connects to the rudder?"

Thankfully, Pilar realized that he wasn't mocking her. Just starting back at the beginning, with something she knew.

"Thank you for getting the compass," Pablo said.

Pilar broke off another piece of orange. "My Uncle Luis got it. He may be the only person in Havana who could deliver such a thing."

Pablo nodded, ready to move on. She was always so proud. Too much pride for her own good. He really didn't want to hear any-more about her fabulous family. If everything was so glorious, what was she doing on a small boat in the Florida Straits with him? Why couldn't her uncle pay the necessary bribes to have her carried across on a cigarette boat out of Miami? He knew why. They didn't have as much money or as many connections as everybody thought.

"Here, you take it," Pablo said and he abruptly let go of the small stick, the tiller that connected to twin rudders that jutted down into the blue-black waters beneath them.

"Wait," she said, dropping the rest of her orange on the white can-vas.

The yellow-white sails flapped in protest as she struggled to put everything right. He let her flounder for awhile before returning his hand back to the tiller. Together they straightened things out and soon were back on course. Good, he told her, and let his hand move away again. He began to eat part of the orange she had dropped.

Pilar could steer pretty well when she concentrated. Around them there was nothing but ocean blue. Cuba had disappeared off the stern and a small chop built out of the west, where a low bank of clouds, almost looking like distant mountains, had now appeared.

"Right now we're steering five to ten degrees west of north."

"West of north?" Pilar exclaimed. "But Florida, the Keys, that is all to the northeast. Don't you remember?"

"Then go ahead," Pablo said. "Steer us east of north, if you want."

There was no telling this woman anything. She was like too many of them. No listen, all talk.

Pilar pulled the tiller toward her, eager to change course to star-board, but as she did so, the sails flapped in protest and the Hobie slowed, beginning to choke like an exhausted horse.

"Here," Pablo said with disgust. He took the tiller from her. "You put us right into the wind. It's called 'in irons.'"

For the first time, she looked around them, at the small pieces of string he had attached to the Hobie's wire shrouds a few weeks ago.

"Remember the string will tell us where the wind is coming from," he said. "Remember, Pilar, the wind is invisible, so we have to use the string, the flecks on the water to tell us which direction it is coming from. I'd love to steer straight to Florida, too, but right now the wind won't let us."

Pilar nodded and he let the tiller pass back to her fingertips. The sun climbed into the sky and Pablo ate the rest of the orange while she steered. She wasn't bad for a beginner. When he sensed that she lost concentration, and they began to list to the left or the right, he returned his hand to the tiller. Just enough to get them back on course, and then he allowed her to continue to steer. "Torpedo runs." That's what Señor Pena used to call such lapses. He was the one who taught Pablo how to sail. He was in charge of the beach at the Cayo Coco until that afternoon the security guards took him away. Some whispered that he had been selling drugs to the tourists on the side. Or he planned to steal one of the boats and escape as they were doing now. Pablo never knew the truth or heard from him again. But he knew that in teaching him how to sail, Señor Pena had revealed how the world really worked. That there were forces out on the ocean that people couldn't see, but anybody can use them to his advantage if he watched and waited for his chance.

Señor Pena taught Pablo that the wind was always shifting. Minute to minute, hour to hour, it never stayed at the same strength or out of the same direction.

"Bigger wind coming," Pilar said and pointed at the clouds beginning to fill the western horizon.

Both of them squinted into that direction. Pilar had grown quiet once again, and it took Pablo a while to realize that she was waiting for him to say something. Waiting to hear what he had decided about the dark, angry clouds that were drawing closer to them.

"Big wind for sure," Pablo said. "Good enough to blow us to Florida in no time."

He prayed that she didn't hear the hesitation that crept into his voice. Eager to change the subject, Pablo asked her the question that he hadn't been able to get out of his head for weeks now.

"Pilar, why did you have to leave?"

"Because I'm like you," she replied. "It was time to leave."

"But if it hadn't been for you, I could have stayed."

She laughed at this. "No, you would have gone some day. The temptation, this boat tied there to the dock, would have been too much for you."

"But you have so much more than me, than most. You're married to—"

"The best ballplayer in Cuba," she said. "The great Omar Silva."

"And that must make your life easier."

"Easier," she nodded, "and harder."

Pilar glanced over one shoulder and now the other. There was nothing but water all around them.

"I know harder doesn't make much sense to somebody like you," Pilar said and she focused upon him for the first time since their voyage had begun. "But the curse of being married to somebody like Omar Silva is that you come to understand how close you are to a completely different life. That is if you dare to take the first step."

Pablo shook his head. "I don't understand."

"A lot of people watch me dance every night. But more watch Omar every time he takes the field. And it's not just the fans. The fans are like the ones who pack the ballroom every night at Cayo Coco. Eyes always wide with wonder. No, there are other ones. Those who send word back to the American teams, the major leagues. Sometimes they will tell my Omar that he's good enough to play for this team or that in *El Norte*. Their talk sometimes drives him crazy. But I tell him to listen, to please God listen."

"Why?"

"Because then he would truly know if he could play with the best. Everybody thinks that when El Duque escaped to the major leagues it was all about the money. How much he could make. But it's something more."

"How could it be more?"

"Pablo, don't be a stupid boy. Don't you see? If you leave then you truly know, especially if you're somebody like Omar or El Duque. You would know exactly where you stand in your world. If you were good enough to play on their ballfield every day. There would be no more questions."

They sailed on and Pablo considered what he had heard. She had never been so open with him.

"You wanted him to leave," he said. "But Omar isn't sure."

She smiled. "You're smarter than you look."

"So maybe you force his hand? If he won't leave, you will. If you get to Florida maybe he has to follow."

"We will see."

Throughout the morning and into the early afternoon they kept on the same heading, north by northwest, angling away from their destination. They took shelter from the sun in the shadow of the mainsail. But by mid-afternoon Pablo decided they needed a course correction. He took the tiller back from her and tacked into the wind.

"What are you doing?" she asked.

He nodded at the clouds. They had become a part of their world now. A low-lying string of angry mountains that perhaps somebody back home could see way out to sea if they were atop one of the high bluffs near the harbor. But they, of course, were no longer home. Near the interior where one could ride out the worst of storms. During the hurricane season, that was where Pablo's mother sometimes took him. To Holguin to see her sister. It was one of the events that the year was planned around. Back when he was very young, when the Russians were still in Cuba and gas was available, they could drive to Holguin in his aunt's old Chevy. But now, in this special time in the period of peace, they would have to wait for the bus or catch a ride with a friend with better connections for gas and meat and a good job.

Pablo handed the tiller back to Pilar and scrambled across the canvas deck to the mast. First he undid the line holding up the jib and let it flutter like a surrender flag down to him. With deft hands, he stuffed the sail into its yellow nylon bag that was tied down to one of the hulls. As he did this, Pablo considered the water slapping off the fiberglass hulls no more than an arm's length from him. They were such a fragile beast out here on this wide, open sea. For the first time he became truly frightened. Not about anybody catching them or what would happen if they did. No, for the first time Pablo became uncertain about what he had gotten himself into. He couldn't decide which entity he was more afraid of—the sea or this woman.

He ratcheted the mainsail down to one-third its full size and tucked away the extra sailcloth with three bungee chords, just as Señor Pena had taught him. Already he could feel the wind shifting as the clouds drew closer. Pablo let out the mainsheet, almost as far as it would go.

Pilar sensed the change in the weather and eagerly held out the tiller for him to take when he returned to the back of the boat. Without having to be told, she moved about the canvas top deck on her hands and knees, tying down the jugs of fresh water, the wooden chest of fruit, crackers, cereal and day-old dinner rolls. Everything they were able to steal away from the Cayo Coco kitchen the last few days. After they had made their decision to finally leave. Pablo saw that she had some sense after all. She had decided to stay as busy as she could. In glancing up at the darkening sky, Pablo knew that he couldn't blame her. The dark clouds were bearing down on them hard.

"I wonder what they're thinking back at Cayo Coco," he said, trying to make small talk. "What they'll say once they realize we're gone."

But Pilar wasn't having any of it.

"Don't you wonder?" he asked when she didn't reply.

"I know," she snapped.

"You just know?"

"They're so predictable, stuck in their ways. I can see it all in my head."

"Then tell me. What are they doing? What will they do?"

Yet she shook him off. For now, she was intent on keeping such memories and visions to herself.

SEVEN

LUIS HATED TO SEE THE MUSICIANS GO. He was so embarrassed with the way they were required to depart Havana this last day. All of them in a single line that stretched from the doors into the terminal, where everyone could gawk at them, even come over and strike up a conversation if they had enough nerve. Back in the United States they wouldn't have to go through something like this. At least not for as long as clearing customs took with only two counters open. Back home they would be ushered to a more private area. Something more befitting of their station in world. But this was Cuba, after all. That was what he would tell them. What can you do, except smile through it?

In the end, the American musicians didn't seem that upset by how they were treated that morning—their last memory of Cuba. Bonnie Raitt smiled at Luis, even though she must have been so tired. After the final concert last night, the party had continued back at the Hotel Nacional and went on all night. Luis never slunk away to get any sleep and he didn't remember Bonnie or many of the other artists leaving, either. They drank and talked and played until the sun rose into a blood-red sky and there was barely enough time to gather up one's things and head to the airport in one of the cars that Luis had provided.

Amy and Emily, the Indigo Girls, were just ahead of Bonnie in line. They were talking with Jimmy Buffett and Peter Frampton.

Bonnie looked over at Luis and waved, with a half-exasperated look on her face. Luis nodded in return. His cars had taken the musicians to Jose Marti International Airport. The government had entrusted him with that service because they knew they wouldn't have to worry with him in charge. Uncle Luis remained a reliable man in an unsettled land, and that would always be a valuable commodity.

Bonnie smiled and turned away. The long line was finally, slowly, moving up, closer to the customs station. Luis loved the way Bonnie's red hair shimmered in the morning light. He decided that Cuba was too hot, too imprecise, for somebody like her. She had told him as much yesterday, while he was making the rounds at the Hotel Nacional, making sure that everyone was happy and everything was taken care of. Bonnie told him that she had grown up in New England.

"It's cold and gray up there," she said and he could tell that she missed it.

To be on the road as much as these musicians, well, few from Cuba could imagine such a thing. To be able to travel and leave to wherever one wanted, whenever one wanted. Luis couldn't decide if that would be a dream or a nightmare.

Later, after the musicians' plane left for Miami, Luis decided he would go home to his two-story flat a few blocks from the Hotel Nacional and the Malecon and look up New England in that old world atlas a friend of his from the city library sold to him. Luis knew that parts of the world had changed so much since the red-bound atlas was printed in 1979. A general in the Soviet army originally gave the volume to the library as a going-away gift. That was what happened to precious things sometimes in Cuba. They fell from hand to hand, never really touching the ground, never truly forgotten. In those pages, the old Soviet Union still existed. But, of course, that empire has been split into Russia and the Ukraine and other countries Luis couldn't remember. But the United States, where Bonnie and the Indigo Girls and the others returned to, that was as constant as a towering rock in the ocean. For any Cuban, the United States was the *El Norte* that overshadowed everything else on the maps of the world.

Luis and his brother Jaime would sometimes play a game where one of them would name a state, such as Montana, and the other would need to answer what the surrounding states were (North Dakota, Washington, Idaho) and then maybe the capital (Helena). Jaime was good at this game, but not as good as Luis.

Before Fidel, people knew much more about the United States, as they did about the world in general. It wasn't unusual for people to honeymoon at Miami or the Florida beaches. Plenty of people bought their first set of silverware from the United States.

In a perfect world, Luis would have arranged for such things when every one of his nieces married. They would have loved nothing better than to honeymoon in Miami, too. Of course, such things were impossible now. The memory remained, but the actual events had moved far out of anybody's control. Still, Luis did what he could. He pulled strings and got that suite at the Habana Libre for Pilar. That was almost as good as any hotel in South Beach Miami. At least that was what the musicians had told him.

Luis enjoyed helping his niece with her wedding. Her Omar seemed to be a decent enough person, for a baseball player. Luis hoped that the marriage would be good for Pilar. She could be so headstrong sometimes.

Bonnie and the others reached the lone checkpoint for customs. Why the government had only two stations open was anybody's guess. With so many people here this morning, it was so embarrassing. Bonnie, bless her, turned and waved one last time in Luis's direction before she disappeared through the doors and out onto the black tarmac. Luis nodded and raised a hand in return. That was so kind of her. He would be sure to mention it if they ever saw each other again.

Luis knew he should leave right away. There was so much to do back at the garage. He needed to make sure the four cars were serviced and ready for a Canadian charter arriving from Toronto tomorrow morning. But these recent events, first the ballgame against the Baltimore Orioles and then the "Bridge to Havana" concert, were such sweet treats that he found that he couldn't just let it all go. He knew it was important that he found a safe place for it in his mind. A room that he could always visit and see Bonnie Raitt's glowing red hair, the Indigo Girls talk and whisper among themselves. A safe place where he could hear them sing and play as they did for the few days when they were here, in his Havana.

At the Hotel Nacional, the musicians were paired up—one American act with one Cuban. The names were drawn out of a hat and afterward they went to their rooms and made music. Enough music for a CD and the concert on the last night of their stay. For some, it didn't work out. But for others, well, it was glorious.

In such moments it somehow fell together. Luis was the one going up and down the back stairs, making sure everyone had what they needed: sodas, ice, rum, cigars. Certainly not an important job, but it allowed him to be where he wanted to be. That had always been important for Luis. To be inside. One of the Nacional rooms was where he first heard Bonnie sing. As soon as he heard that voice, the way it could be smooth one moment, rough and angry the next, he pulled up a chair and listened. Listened hard. Because he knew that something like this came into a person's life only a few times before they nailed down the coffin lid for good.

For this was what didn't reach Cuba anymore—here behind the curtain that separated the island from the rest of the world. Some said that all a Cuban needed was the baseball highlights from Miami, Telemundo, and the other American stations that people stole into hotels to catch a glimpse of. Sometimes in Cuba it was better to have a relative working at the Nacional or the Libre than to have a doctor in the family. A relative in the tourist trade, even a maid or a busboy, could sneak someone inside for a few precious moments of television. View the whole world laid out in front of them.

Almost all the musicians had made it through customs now, and Luis thought of staying until the planes took off for Miami. But he realized that would only make him sadder. Perhaps it was a good thing that Pilar wasn't here, with him, this morning. She would have seen a famous face or two, but when she couldn't join them on the other side of customs? Yes, that would have just made her angry all over again. Deep down, Luis couldn't blame her. It wasn't right. A sense of injustice hung over this land and somehow his favorite niece refused to accept it.

Back outside Luis put on his sunglasses. Ray-Bans left in one of his cars during the week. He liked to imagine that they were Bonnie's.

He got in the Audi and started it up. The Corolla, the old Chevy, and the Land Rover should already be back at the garage. His boys knew that. No *joy-riding*, another American word, not today. Not with that big charter from Toronto coming in.

Luis's garage was down an alleyway in Miramar. The new hotels were visible above the squat houses and apartments. Even though Luis couldn't glimpse the ocean from here, the blue waters were near-by. At the shop he used his other senses—the salt smell, the frigate birds flying overhead—to remind himself that the beach was only a short walk away.

When Luis arrived at the garage, he found his brother, Jaime, waiting for him. Jaime leaned against the polished front bumper of his Honda. Around him Luis's men worked in the small yard and the nearby cement-block garage. Jaime stood and brushed off his pants as Luis approached.

"She's gone," he said.

"Who's gone?"

Luis looked past his older brother and told Ortega to change the oil in this one, too. Be quick about it because Luis would need the vehicle later this afternoon.

"Pilar."

"Pilar," Luis repeated and focused on his brother for the first time. "Jaime, here, let's get a coffee. I don't understand you."

"Pilar," Jaime said. "Pilar is gone. They say," he looked around and then whispered, "she defected."

"Defected? But how?"

Luis put an arm over his brother's bony shoulders and steered him back toward his car. Sometimes the way Jaime blurted out things, well, it could be too dangerous.

"Start at the beginning," Luis told him.

"She didn't show up at work this morning," Jaime said. "Maria's friend, that Elena, told us. She pointed out that Omar's gone with the baseball team. He won't be back until after the game in Baltimore."

"All right, but what about Pilar?"

"The last time anybody at Cayo Coco saw her was after the fi-nal show last night. Pilar was supposed to be back at the resort this morning. To help divide up what the tourists left behind. That Loot Party they always have."

"So, she didn't feel like going?"

"No, Luis, there's more," Jaime said. "The kid who ran the small marina is gone, too. So is a new sailboat, something called a Hobie Cat."

"And people think they left together? On a sailboat?"

Jaime nodded. "From what Elena says, the boat's barely bigger than a car. But this boy, Pablo's his name, he is a good sailor."

"But there's nothing to say that Pilar went with him."

"Elena says the two of them—Pilar and this boy—were good friends."

***

Jaime and Luis drove out to the Cayo Coco in the Audi, one of the company cars. Luis had insisted upon that. His brother couldn't afford any more trouble with his vehicle. Even though it was less than forty-five minutes from the city, the resort was like another world. Out here the beaches glimmered in the afternoon sun and Luis silently promised himself that he would start coming out this way more often. His cars and drivers saw much of this and he decided he should, too. After all, he was the boss. He couldn't let the hired help have all of the fun.

"I wonder if Omar knows," Jaime said. "If this is some plan for the two of them to escape?"

Luis's brother was the taller of the two, but he didn't carry himself well. God in heaven, the way he walked through life it was like he was trying to hide, Luis thought. Even now, Luis noticed that Jaime sat hunched forward in the tan leather seat, trying to keep his head from blowing in the wind.

Luis asked, "You think Omar's looking to leave as well?"

Jaime shrugged. The national team had left for Baltimore last night. The game was the day after tomorrow. But the more Luis considered all this, the more he wondered.

Luis had gone to the Orioles game in Havana. Usually tickets were free—first come, first serve. But for the contest against the big leaguers, the Baltimore Orioles, only party regulars and sport federation people were allowed into the old ballpark in Havana. Luis knew that to Jaime and the rest of the family it made perfect sense that he, the little brother, would be there. After all, wasn't Luis always at the most exciting events in Havana? What his big brother didn't know was that to do both things—the Orioles game and the "Bridge to Havana" concert—Luis had had to pull every string he could.

Except for an occasional lorry and tourist bus, they were the only car on the road. At the bus stops, long lines waited in the shade. The people glared at the two brothers in the shining car as it passed by. If they weren't in a hurry, Luis told himself, they would have stopped. Given some poor soul a ride. That's just good *karma*. Another American word he had learned in recent years.

"It's funny," Jaime said. "At the reception, at the Libre, Omar told me he was getting out of the return trip to Baltimore. The best man, you remember him?"

"Carmelo Rodriguez."

"That's him. Omar was talking about him taking his place. Omar didn't want to go. He'd had enough of the Orioles. But both of them went. At least that's what I heard."

Luis accelerated. Up ahead of them was the guardhouse for Cayo Coco.

"They'd want Omar to play against the Orioles again," Luis said. "He's their best player. I wouldn't be surprised if that directive came from Fidel himself."

After signing in, they passed through the white-silver-colored gates for Cayo Coco that towered into the blue sky.

"The gates of heaven," Jaime said and then tried to laugh. "That's what Pilar calls them."

Inside they are directed to the hotel director, Asafa Lyons. He greeted them, all smiles and handshakes in his office that overlooked a diamond-shaped pool. The Germans had built this particular resort. It started to come back to Luis as they lit up Minero cigars and tried to carry on as if they were such good friends. The government must get a third off the top, easy, Luis figured.

"All I know is that nobody's seen her or the boy since last night," Asafa said. He was a hulking man with rich black skin. Luis couldn't immediately place the name, but then it came to him. The beast had been in the Olympics years ago. He'd done well, too. Silver or bronze medal in the two-hundred meters. So, this was where he had landed. What the party had done to reward him.

"But why put her and this boy together?" Luis asked. "That could simply be coincidence. That she and the boy are both away today."

"Normally, I'd agree," Asafa said and he leaned back in his leather office chair. He inhaled the rich smoke like a greedy man. He waited a moment, letting the smoke curl out of nostrils that could belong to a bear or a lion in the wild.

"Yes, normally, there would no reason to jump to conclusions," Asafa said. "But several of us have noticed that she's been going down to the marina more and more in recent weeks. In fact, nobody can remember her ever straying far from the hotel until a few weeks ago. Pilar would stay with Luz and the other girls from the show. But she seems to have fallen into some new habits, new infatuations."

That was nothing but gossip and conjecture. Luis was tempted to say such a thing aloud. But he knew they must play the game. Act as if they're all *compadres* in this nasty excuse for a country.

"Can we take a look at the marina?" Luis asked and Jaime appeared surprised.

"If you'd like," Asafa said. "Please, follow me."

Puffing on their cigars, the three of them walked down a white-marble spiral staircase and passed through the lobby of more white marble and beneath a grand crystal chandelier. Jaime was stunned by the majesty of the place. It was as ornate as the Nacional and Libre downtown. Luis could feel the anger swelling inside himself and once again he tried to understand how Castro could ask the people to come to work in a palace like this and then have them return home at night to cement-block hovels and tin-roofed hunts? It was a cruel joke. Pilar certainly had it better than most. Luis had to believe she knew that. But how do you live in a world that reminds you every day that there can be so much more?

As the three of them walked down to the marina, Luis feared that he had helped push everything in the wrong direction. That in giving Pilar as much as he could, in pulling strings to have her wedding reception in a place as grand as Libre, in getting her a job in a resort like this, he had only underscored the lie, the disconnect, about their homeland. That there could be more. That there should be more.

"Here we are," Asafa said when they reached the end of the board-walk and the small lagoon. "It isn't much, but the tourists like it."

What was not to like? There were several jet-skis and smaller sail-boards—all easily led out to the beach and the glittering wide sea. There was little surf today and the white sand stretched as far as the eye could see to the right and back toward a breakwater in the distance to the left.

"The empty spot, the other side of the dock," Asafa says. "That's where the Hobie boat should be."

He flicked what was left of his cigar into the shallow water. The new charters of tourists would arrive this afternoon and Luis knew that before then some poor soul would have to fish the boss man's cigar butt out of the lagoon.

Jaime asked, "Could such a boat make it across, to the United States?"

It was a good question and it surprised Luis that his brother would have the balls to ask it.

Asafa shrugged again, briefly stretching the collar of his Cayo Coco polo shirt.

"How would I know?" he answered with a smile. "I've never thought of such a thing. I'm happy in my country."

Of course, that was Fidel and the party talking. Words that haven't done them any good in many years. But like foolish children they had little choice but to nod along with reverence at such nonsense, and that was exactly what Luis and Jaime did.

"Thank you," Luis said. "Thank you for your time."

Then the men shook hands all around.

On the way home, Luis took the local road along the ocean to Havana, and he and his brother stole glances at the water, as if they could see Pilar and this boy. Out there. Beyond the breakers.

Luis dropped off his brother back at the shop and made sure that

Jaime headed directly home to Maria. His boys had done a good job. Everything was ready for tomorrow and Luis headed for home himself. When Luis got to his two-bedroom flat, he knew he should pray to Changó at the altar he had set up in the small corner of his living room. He knew he needed to burn as many candles as he could find to help his niece in her passage.

But he didn't stay at the flat for long. It was there that he remembered the compass. One of the many requests Pilar made of him in recent months. The wedding rings, the room at the Habana Libre. He had forgotten about the compass, something he saw as nothing more than a memento for her new husband. That's how she had framed it. A curious knick-knack between lovers. But now Luis realized that Omar had never received that gift. The compass was for her escape.

At dusk, Luis walked the breakwater of old stones that marked the channel between Miramar and Havana. There he sat until his eyes ached from staring out at the sea. He decided he wouldn't tell his brother about the compass.

Sitting there, Luis tried to be angry about what had happened. But deep in his heart, he found that such fury had left him. All he could do was gaze at the darkening waters and know that his beloved niece, his Pilar, was gone.

EIGHT

THE WAVES CAME AT THEM IN STEADY ROWS that built in violence. They reminded Pablo of the military marches at the Plaza de Revolution beneath the dark-stone mural of comrade Che. Row after row of numbing power that frequently occurred back when he was a child and the Soviets were still with them. His mother had never trusted the Russians. "They cannot dance," she once whispered to him. "Not like us." But that didn't keep her from allowing his father to take him to the May Day ceremonies. In looking back on it, those were the best days he spent with his father. The times when the older man was genuinely interested in what he had to say, what he wanted to do with his life. Soon after the Soviets left for good, his father disappeared from their lives. He had fallen in with one of the women who worked at the old Soviet embassy, back when it was filled with people from Russia, their new comrades. Father had been a driver for the embassy. Back and forth to the airport, taking Russian officials around town. One thing led to another. That's how his aunt had put it to Pablo. One thing led to another, and now his father lived in Moscow or St. Petersburg. Occasionally he called home.

The dividing line between the sky and the sea was soon lost to them. The waves continued to build as Pablo pulled down more of the yellow-silver sails, except for a glimmer of the bigger one—the mainsail.

"What are you doing?" Pablo asked.

He hesitated before answering. How to explain that soon everything would come crashing down on them and he only wanted enough sail area to give him some maneuverability.

"This is how Señor Pena told me to do it," he said.

"Who?"

"Señor Pena. The old man who taught me how to sail."

"The one they arrested?"

"He could have escaped," Pablo says, "if he wanted."

"Pablo? Is this another fairy tale of yours?"

A large whitecap, the biggest wave yet, broke over the canvas that stretched between the two glistening hulls. Silently they watched the water race across the deck.

Pilar reached for the small compass, still encased in the wooden box that it came in. She slipped her hand lovingly under its cool brass. It almost fit fully in her fist. As Pablo watched her, she tucked it into a front pocket of her cut-off jeans.

Pablo saw that he would have to be the strong one now. The woman had the wild look of fear growing in her eyes. As the sea began to rage around them, the skies opened up and within minutes they were soaked to the bone, their hair hugging their skulls. Both of them sat on the canvas deck, hunched over at the waist, preparing for the worst.

"Pilar," Pablo called out above the din of the rain.

"What?" she answered.

"Señor Pena could have escaped," the boy said. "I know it."

Another wave broke over the deck, and Pilar reached out, hanging onto one of the metal wires that led up to the mast.

"Pablo, do you think they miss us yet?"

"Miss us?" the boy answered as the wind began to howl.

"Know that we're gone," Pilar said, drawing closer to him, trying to imagine that he was bigger in frame and stature, big enough to shield her.

"I don't know," Pablo replied.

"They do," Pilar said, her voice becoming strained, more ragged in the wind. "I know exactly what they would do. It's like I told you. I can picture it all in my mind."

NINE

THE NEXT MORNING JAIME CAME BY THE SHOP, bright and early, driving his beloved Honda. He waited until Luis sent the fleet of four cars and the mini-bus to the airport to greet the charter from Toronto. Luis had planned to go with his men. But when he looked at his brother, his skinny frame resting against the front bumper, he decided that his guys could do the job on their own. As the fleet exited the fenced-in compound, he walked over to his brother's car.

"Where to?" Luis said as he opened the passenger door.

"That's what I'm asking *you*."

They sat there for a moment, Jaime behind the wheel, the key back in the ignition.

"Alberto's."

Jaime shook his head, but he started up the car.

"I know you don't want to go there," Luis said, "but you have to agree that Alberto is the best place to start."

Jaime didn't answer. Instead he stared straight ahead, both hands gripping the wheel at the ten and two positions, and began to drive in the direction of the Malecon. It was like any other day in Havana: rollers from the deep sea struck the breakwater that ran along the edge of the old city. Occasionally spray from those waves flew over them. Rain on a day of nothing but blue skies. If tourists had been in his car, Jaime knew that they would have laughed and talked too excitedly for him to really understand what they were saying. The spray along the Malecon? It was like an amusement park ride. That's what one of them, maybe that Canadian businessman who always had his arm around the woman who smelled of jasmine, once said. To a visitor like that Canadian, waves hitting the Malecon seawall were like everything else that Cuba exhibited or possessed: simply held out for the rest of the world's enjoyment.

But today, when another wave hit the giant stone wall, Jaime tensed up. Those were big rollers. God, how he hoped his Pilar wasn't out in that.

"You know I'm right, don't you?" his brother said again. "Alberto, the old general, he may have heard something."

Still, Jaime didn't answer. Instead he drove for the tunnel that would take them under the harbor and to the fortress that stood up on the bluffs. Alberto had been there during the tribunals—when Che ordered thousands to die by firing squad. If it had been Jaime, he would have moved as far away as he could after such times. But Alberto still lived nearby. The old fortress that looked down over the entrance to the harbor had become a museum with ample enough space to hold an annual book fair and the *Bienal de la Habana,* the big art exhibition. Alberto now worked as a tour guide at the old fort—something Jaime couldn't decide was mere circumstance or a cruel joke.

After he parked the car in the lot alongside a shiny tourist bus, Jaime and his brother walked across the stone bridge over a small moat to the entrance. There they found Alberto in the office that Che Guevara had once occupied.

"My niece is missing," Luis began and Jaime found that he was grateful that his brother had said niece instead of my brother's daughter or something more accusatory, perhaps more accurate.

"Pilar, right?" Alberto said while flipping through a stack of papers on his desk. "The one who married the baseball player?"

Luis nodded and Jaime struggled to reply, "That's right."

At the crack in Jaime's voice, Alberto peered up and finally remembered his manners.

"Please, please, sit down, my friends," he said.

Jaime and Luis each settled into tall, straight chairs across from Alberto. The chairs were dark wood with many coats of varnish, and Jaime wondered how long these pieces of furniture had been around. Did they date back to Che and the tribunals and the firing squads?

"She's not listed here," Alberto said and pushed the short stack of official reports to one side. "Sometimes we don't receive the latest paperwork. We are a museum after all."

"Is there somebody else, in the government, we should talk to?" Luis asked.

Alberto shook his head, like a headmaster disappointed with a student's recitation.

"No, leave that do me," he said. His voice was a low growl, like pebbles falling on a dirt country road. "Things are difficult right now."

With that Alberto briefly tapped one shoulder. The sign of the man who always wore a military uniform with epaulets. Jaime almost expected him to stroke an imaginary beard. Another sign of Fidel Castro. That their leader had become like a crazy uncle that nobody was sure how to approach or how to control anymore. Jaime couldn't believe that it had come to this. That someone still as powerful as Alberto Sanchez was afraid of Fidel, too.

"The best thing you two can do is talk with friends of the family, friends of hers," Alberto said. "Make the rounds. Perhaps somebody has heard something of consequence."

"But Alberto—" Luis said.

Yet the old general momentarily raised both hands as if in surrender.

"You do what you can and I'll do the same," Alberto said. "It is better this way."

Somewhere out on the grounds, the commotion of a tourist group drew closer. Alberto stood and pulled the front of his European dress shirt taunt, ridding it of any wrinkles.

"I'll let you know if I hear anything," he said.

Outside, the two brothers walked back down the small rise to the parking lot.

"Well?" Jaime said.

"Let's do as the old man said," Luis replied. "We'll make a day out of it."

***

From the old fortress, Jaime drove back through the tunnel that ran two thousand feet under Rio Almendares. Coming back up into the light and traffic, the car briefly flirted with other vehicles heading up the Malecon toward the Hotel Nacional and the low-slung buildings and resorts of Miramar. But Jaime adeptly angled the car across busy lanes, eliciting a brief clamor of horns, until he swung a sharp left onto El Prado. The Capitolio dome rose in the distance.

"Stop up here," Luis said.

"Where?"

"Mineros. The cigar shop."

"I don't believe you sometimes, brother."

"What?"

"Pilar is gone and you're buying more cigars for your tourist friends."

"Mineros is a place for gossip, too. Maybe somebody has heard something."

"Believe that if you want," Jaime said and pulled the car over to the curb.

"Fine then. Don't come in."

"I'm not," Jaime said pulling the hand brake with an extra tug.

"Then where are you going?"

"The seminary. To see Father Jose. He knows as much as anybody in your cigar store."

"Okay, then," Luis said. "I'll meet you back here in a half-hour."

A bell above the door at Mineros jingled as Luis entered. The room smelled of sweet tobacco and damp wood. Nobody was in the reading chair that sat atop a small platform in front of the work stations. Thank God, Luis told himself. If anybody spouted party dogma to him right now, the glory of Fidel and socialism, he was liable to take a swing at them. Only a few chairs in the four rows of dark tables were occupied.

"Luis," said Gloria, a large woman with thick eyeglasses held together by scotch tape. "You need more? You were just here last week."

"Gloria, you should have seen those Americans," he replied. "The musicians down at the Nacional. They couldn't get enough of your

Churchills. One of them, she was going to write a song to your cigars."

"Which singer?"

"A really good one," Luis said. "She plays guitar, too. Her name is Bonnie."

"I've never heard of her," Gloria said and crinkled her nose, almost in disgust.

Luis nodded as he if expected this response. For that was the state of affairs here in Cuba, he thought. We know nothing of what the rest of the world listens to, what they have come to embrace as their own.

"I need another three dozen Churchills," Luis said. "The long ones."

He pointed at the cartons behind the glass case that stood between them.

"They are your favorites, too," Gloria said.

They are the world's favorites, Luis almost said. He knew that he must have handed out thousands over the years. He watched as Gloria wrapped the slender cigars in brown paper.

"My niece, my favorite niece, is missing," he said in a low voice, so the others, the ones working at rolling more cigars, couldn't hear him. His voice was barely audible over the rustle of the paper. Gloria paused and leaned closer to listen.

"I'm sorry," she replied, not looking up.

"Her name is Pilar," Luis continued, noting that the mention of his niece's name caused no ripple of recognition on the old woman's weathered face.

"She worked at Cayo Coco, out at the beach."

The old woman fastened the final loose tab of brown paper down with a short piece of yellow tape.

"Pilar," Gloria said and held the package of cigars out to him. "I'll let you know if I hear anything."

***

Jaime and Father Rinaldo sat in the courtyard of San Carlos Seminary drinking tea. Here was where Jaime had once studied before Maria came into his life. He couldn't help wondering how his life would have been different if he hadn't seen Maria that one night, in the bar down in the old part of the city, not far from the Floritida. He usually didn't go to bars, but he had gone that night because others from his squadron were going out. They talked him into it.

"Do you think they have run off?" Father Rinaldo asked.

Jaime shook his head. "It doesn't make sense. Omar is getting ready to play the Americans again."

"But this time they are playing in the United States, right?" Father Rinaldo said. "In Baltimore? Perhaps Omar and Pilar planned—" Here the good father stopped. The old man Jaime had known since he was teenage boy looked around them, even though there was nobody nearby. Only the colonnaded passageways that surrounded them on four sides and the low-lying fronds of ferns and palm trees. They were very much alone, but still Father Rinaldo hesitated before going on.

"They could have worked out an arrangement," he whispered.

And for the time since Jaime had heard the news that Pilar had disappeared, he felt happy. A warm feeling swelled up inside him.

"It is possible," he replied, so wanting to believe Father Rinaldo. "Yes, maybe they are up to something."

After that Jaime and Father Rinaldo sipped their hot tea and gazed up at the cloudless sky set in a perfect square by the courtyard perimeter. It was good to feel at peace, to simply let things go and allow God to guide one's hand, Jaime decided. He and the good priest exchanged a few more words before saying goodbye.

As Jaime kissed Father Rinaldo's hand, he murmured that he would visit again.

"Soon," he said.

Outside, Jaime's brother was waiting by the car.

"You should have come in," Jaime said, eager to divulge Father Rinaldo's insight. His belief that Pilar and Omar could have somehow run off together. Planned all of this. But Luis's mind was elsewhere.

"We're being followed," Luis said.

Jaime started to look around, but Luis tapped his forearm.

"No, don't," he warned.

"Are you sure?" Jaime said.

"Of course, I'm sure," Luis replied. "Come on. I've got an idea."

They got in the car with Jaime back behind the wheel. As they drove back toward the Malecon, Luis stole glances in the rearview mirror. He ordered his brother to turn left and another sharp left until they swept past the Capitolio, the Prado, and the Hotel Inglaterra. Jaime drove on, faster now, following Luis's directions, until they pulled up in front of the Presidential Palace.

"What are we doing here?"

Luis smiled. "Showing what good patriots we are," he said.

They parked and got out. Side by side the two brothers walked past the revolutionary-era green tank on a stone platform and up the white marble steps, between the square columns and beneath the cupola to the entrance. Between 1920 and 1959, the year of the revolution, the palace had been home to Cuba's presidents.

"Mothers used to talk about when Batista was here," Jaime said. "That Tiffany's decorated everything inside, even the curtains."

The two brothers filed past the life-sized wax figures of Che and Camillo in their guerrilla fatigues and headed upstairs to the exhibits of 1957, the year students stormed the palace, eager to bring Batista to justice. The brothers fell in with the small group of tourists inspecting documents and artifacts from the revolution now enshrined in a waist-high showcase.

Luis kept glancing over his shoulder.

"So who's following us?" Jaime asked.

"Quiet," Luis answered. "He's in a dark suit, driving a new Honda. He's been watching us since the cigar shop. He saw you visit Father Rinaldo."

"That's not a bad thing."

"Brother, visiting a man of the cloth isn't a good thing anymore either, you know that."

Jaime turned to look back. "I don't see anybody," he said.

"Don't do that," Luis said and steered his brother back around to face the exhibits. "Just pretend that you're enthralled by this crap."

They found themselves standing in front of photographs from the assault on the Moncada Barracks in 1953. Many of the student revolutionaries were captured and then brutally tortured: eyes plucked out, faces mutilated.

"I can't look at anymore of this," Jaime said.

They went out the back entrance to the old palace and strolled in the grassy area that used to be the gardens. Up on blocks sat the yacht *Granma*. Every schoolchild in Cuba knew the story of how Fidel and Che and their ragtag army sailed from Mexico aboard this pleasure craft in an operation as ill-conceived as the uprising at Moncada. Government troops were waiting for the boat called *Granma* when it beached on the eastern end of the island. Only eleven revolutionaries, Fidel and Che among them, made it out alive. Three years later they took over the country.

"How lucky can a man be?" Jaime said gazing up at the old yacht.

"I thought the same thing when we first came here as kids," Luis said. "Remember how we were dressed in white shirts, gray shorts, and those red bandannas? So eager to be revolutionaries ourselves."

They turned for the parking lot when Luis stopped dead in his tracks.

"It's him," he muttered under his breath.

"What?" Jaime said. But the man in the suit, his young face so earnest, already stood in front of them.

"Luz," he said.

"Luz?" Luis repeated.

"Luz," the guy said. "She sent me to find you. She has to see you."

"Who are you?"

"Her brother, Tomas."

Luis and Jaime fell in beside the younger man, one brother on either side, as they hurriedly returned to the parking lot.

"We'll follow you," Jaime said when they reached the cars.

Tomas opened the door to his new Honda.

"Why are you dressed like that?" Luis asked. "Dressed so well?"

The question momentarily baffled and then embarrassed the younger man. He gazed down at his shiny new suit. He ran a hand down one lapel as if he couldn't believe that he was in possession of such fine clothing.

"I work at the new dealership," he said. "I have to wear it. They bought it for me."

Luz lived just off the plaza near the old cathedral. Luis could have found it with his eyes closed if the kid had told them the address. But that's not how Tomas wanted it done. He insisted upon leading them slowly through the twisting backstreets a few blocks inland from the Malecon.

"He doesn't trust us," Luis said to his brother.

"Nobody trusts anybody," Jaime replied as they pulled up in front of a three-story, white-stone apartment building a few blocks from the Parque Central. Up the street, kids played baseball. All activity paused for a moment as the brothers got out of the car. A few faces were seen in upstairs bedrooms—everybody checking them out. But, thankfully, regular life picked back up again with the cries of children playing ball and adults going about their business. It was just Luz's brother and two older men, probably from Cayo Coco.

***

Luz was waiting for them upstairs. She was a big girl. Bigger than Pilar. Wide in the carriage and with good-sized breasts. For Luz was the kind of dancer a choreographer routinely puts off to the side or in the second row to highlight the better-looking ones. She was not of middle frame quality, like Pilar. Maybe it was her eyes, the overall angles of her long, almost horse-like face. Luz, bless her heart, didn't look as intelligent, even as mischievous as Pilar. Luz appeared to be the kind of girl who was in trouble before she ever realized it.

Luz heated water for coffee on a hot plate. Jaime declined her offer, but Luis found that he wanted nothing more than a cup of *café con leche*. The girl nodded in agreement and Luis eyed her generous backside as she turned away from them to mix the cups.

"Sit down," she said. "It'll be ready in a minute."

Luis reluctantly moved out of the small kitchen and joined his brother at the table against the far wall. When Luz returned, she had Luis's coffee, as well as several pieces of paper, folded over once and then twice, in her hand.

"These are from Pilar," Luz said. "I found them on my dressing table last night. They were well hidden. They had to be there a day or more."

She held the papers out to the two brothers and, when Jaime refused to move a muscle, Luis accepted them from her. Their fingers briefly touched, and Luz was so warm, like she was on fire. Carefully, with his brother watching, Luis unfolded the pieces of Cayo Coco stationary.

"I didn't want Asafa to find them," Luz said.

"Good," Luis replied and saw that the girl blushed at the attention. What she needs is a good man, Luis thought. Somebody who will really take care of her. With that he began to read:

Dearest Luz:

It falls to you to tell the others. I'm sorry about that, but we need to flee. Asafa is becoming suspicious and Pablo—

Jamie interrupted. "The boy at the boats?"

Luz nodded.

—Pablo says the winds and tides are right for tonight, so we must go. Find my parents and Uncle Luis. Tell them that we've decided to sail this boat called a Hobie for America. Tell them to pray for me. I'll make it to America and then I'll send for you. I'll make the big money and bring over everybody.

Affectingly yours,

Pilar

The room grew quiet and Luis refolded the papers. The letter itself was only a page long. The other blank papers had been folded around it in effort to shield it. For a moment he didn't know what to do with the letter. He certainly wasn't going to let Luz hang on to it. Undoubtedly, the girl would let it slip into the wrong hands. Then he wondered if it was truly safe with him.

The others watched as he reached into his pants pocket and pulled out the gold-plated lighter a Venezuelan client had given him. The same lighter he was lighting the cigars of the rock stars at the Hotel Nacional during the past week. With a flick of the thumb, the flame roared to life, and Luis gingerly held the note over the flame until it ignited. Then he stood and moved past the girl to hold the flame over her sink of dirty dishes. He turned the paper deftly as it turned to ash. Spinning it in his fingertips, Luis waited until he was sure all of it would burn away. Then he dropped what was left in the sink where it landed with a defiant hiss.

"It's our secret now," he told the others.

***

That evening Luis went by the old writer's house. The place was a museum now, with tours given thrice daily by the local home guard. Several of the musicians had visited the one-story house during their long weekend in Havana. The last weekend he had seen his favorite niece.

Luis stopped his car in front of the house and walked up the stone steps to the door. Everything was closed. Shielding his face with both hands, Luis gazed inside and saw the old man's small desk with its Royal typewriter. He never knew why his brother and Maria had named their oldest after the old man's boat. His brother had never been much of a reader, so that couldn't be it. But the name, Pilar, did roll off the tongue. It had to be a name Jaime had heard while driving a visitor out to this tourist stop. That's the way it was with his brother. A word stuck in his head and that was it.

Luis turned and looked at the dark street and the lights of Havana glowing in the distance before returning to his car. Pilar would survive the crossing or die in the attempt. Either way, she was lost to him for a long time, perhaps forever.

TEN

WELL PAST MIDNIGHT, THE HOBIE CAPSIZED. Even though Pablo had stripped away all the sails by then, sacrificed any hope of speed or direction, it wasn't enough to keep the boat upright. With a loud groan, the aluminum mast, as tall as a house back in Cuba, pitched forward into the rising water. Waves rose around them. What was left of the bigger sail, the mainsail, disappeared into dark waters. The last thing Pablo heard before hitting the water was the scream of the metal-wire rigging being ripped away from the two hulls. Water poured in from all sides, sloshing angrily over what was left of the Hobie. "Die," it sang to them. "Just die."

The boy appeared grateful to meet his end, but Pilar would have none of it. As they bobbed to the surface, she grabbed his arm high, near the shoulder. About the only place he had any meat on his bones. And together they struggled to reach one of the hulls. The water pushed against them like a large crowd after a game at the old ballpark. But, eventually, they grasped one hull and what was left of the canvas deck. Everything—the water, food—was gone.

Pablo's hair was swept back from his face, and his dark eyes had grown huge and afraid. Still, he had enough sense to wrap a line around his waist and secure the other end to the edge of the canvas deck. Unable to talk above the wind, he signaled for Pilar to do the same.

"Together," he yelled to the showgirl.

But Pilar could not make out the words.

"Together," Pablo screamed to the heavens, and for the first time both of them realized that they had truly cast themselves beyond the power of Fidel, the inertia that had become Cuba. The ocean, the world itself, had become angry by what they had done.

ELEVEN

THE BALTIMORE ORIOLES had left behind many of their major-league bats and balls as gifts after the game in Havana. They did so as if they expected Team Cuba to put such treasures in a trophy case. Pray to them as natives would to graven images. But the Cuban ballplayers had practiced for the last month with the regulation balls. They had swung the wooden bats instead of aluminum ones used for Olympic and international play. We've taken their gifts, Omar Silva thought as he gazed out of the third-base dugout at the capacity crowd in Baltimore, and learned much from the Americans' foolish charity.

Team Cuba had waited an hour for the drizzle to stop and the exhibition game to finally begin. No matter when the Orioles scored two runs in the first inning off Jose Contreras, Cuba's starting pitcher. The rumor had it that he would sneak away when nobody was looking. The team hotel down by the Baltimore harbor was surrounded with Yanquis waving the Cuban ballplayers to come ever closer. The agent that Pilar had told Omar to look for was there—Rene Tovar. He had winked at Omar from across the street last night. Even from a distance, the gold bracelet and the chains around his neck sparkled from the glow of a streetlight. He watched the slugger's every move. Ready, if Omar was.

Some teams would have hung their heads after falling behind early. But Team Cuba wasn't like most ballclubs. There was talk that Baltimore would put its best pitcher up against Team Cuba. After all, Contreras was the island's best and the Orioles could have started Mike Mussina, their ace. Instead, Omar and company faced somebody named Scott Kamieniecki. The Cuban coaches had never heard of him. Later it was learned that this Kamieniecki was coming back from an injury and was only pitching against Team Cuba to get back into shape.

Omar returned to the dugout after driving Andy Morales in with a double. Cuba had retaken the lead and nearly batted around in the second inning. How Omar wished they could have played a better major league team. Really shown the world how good they were. Out there, between the lines, on that shimmering emerald-green field, Omar had never felt better. In that way, the major leagues indeed were like heaven, and maybe Pilar was right. To play every day in places like this, with the best equipment in the world, never having to worry about whom Fidel would pull off or put on the national team— well, that would be a relief. He saw now that's why Pilar had insisted that he make this trip. Somehow she knew how enthralling this sight would be. How he would want to stay.

Still, Omar wished his beautiful wife had seen what it was like coming to this Camden Yards. If being out on that field was heaven, the rest of this country could be hell. Hours before game time a crowd of several hundred was present, eager to jeer Team Cuba. If Pilar had seen that maybe she would have understood what Omar couldn't seem to ever really explain to her: That in the end, perhaps everyone was better off in their own land, even if the country had fallen upon hard times. Omar could play in these major leagues. He was as sure of it as these Orioles were arrogant. But what would he do the rest of the time in this United States of America? How could he and Pilar exist amid the commotion and boasting of this land, this Camden Yards?

Omar tried to imagine what it would like to live here, in Baltimore, as he took up his position at third base. In the crowd, the large block of fans that had been chanting "USA, USA" was silent now. In the upper deck along the first-base line, he noticed a smaller group yelling "Viva Cuba." A few of them were ringing cowbells. For the first time on this two-day trip, home didn't seem so far away.

Sometimes baseball can be all business and no forgiveness. Fear that the ball will be hit to you and sure enough a bad chopper, with plenty of top spin, will come bouncing your way on the next swing. But take a few deep breaths, believe that things will eventually work out, and time and circumstance could become more generous than many imagined. Under these bright lights, focusing only on the pitcher and the batter, Omar began to feel that he could do this. Maybe Pilar was right. Maybe he could find the courage to defect and she would eventually follow him to this land. Maybe her Uncle Luis would help with this, too, even though Omar didn't see how. Even in Cuba there were limits to what a man with connections like her Uncle Luis could do. At the last Olympics, the western reporters had teased Omar after he made the mistake of telling them about the new car the sports federation had given him—a '61 Chevrolet.

"Omar, can you say Mercedes-Benz, Corvette, 280Z?" they said.

While he knew that there were newer, much fancier cars in the world, he wondered if that was reason enough to leave a country, probably forever. Omar almost asked those reporters that question, but he knew it would only be misunderstood and make trouble for himself.

At the crack of the bat, a hard grounder shot up the third-base line. It skimmed across the grass once, twice, and Omar glided toward it, positioning himself as best he could. He flipped the glove to the backhand side and felt the ball jump up, snared in the webbing. In one motion, he planted his right foot and reached into the glove. He fired the ball across the diamond to get the Oriole base runner by a half-step.

That was the third out of the inning and as Team Cuba ran off the field, here and there, in the crowd, people began to applaud. Some of them even stood.

"Omar Silva," the PA announcer said for no apparent reason and the applause built a bit more before fading away above the glowing lights of the city.

Team Cuba filed into the dugout, leaving their gloves on the steps or flipping them onto the small shelf atop the bench. One of the coaches barked the batting order, when it happened. If two or three men got on, Omar would bat this inning. It was the ordinary business of baseball when a loud cheer rose from the crowd and Omar's team turned to see three people running onto the field—two adults and a teenager. One carried a Cuban flag and the kid a Free Cuba sign. The Cuban ballplayers watched as the security police moved in from the sidelines.

"Idiots," somebody said and the team tried to focus on the next at-bat.

Omar wondered if Pilar, even Carmelo, would consider these demonstrators as idiots. Carmelo wasn't at the game. Word had it that they had locked him in his room at the Hyatt Hotel. That he had been too talkative about his possible plans to defect. So now he was in the worst of all worlds. He couldn't play and would be going home to an uncertain future. Once again Omar told himself not to become too caught up in such things. If you're going to do something totally crazy like defect, keep your mouth shut. When you start thinking such thoughts, nobody is your friend.

Team Cuba tacked on two more runs and then held the Orioles scoreless in the bottom of the fourth inning. The major leaguers seemed partly embarrassed, partly bored. For Team Cuba, this was the biggest game in the world. But the Baltimore team had supposedly wanted the day off. They were looking forward to playing golf, being home with their families. That's what Omar's manager had told his team.

Once more the stands swelled with noise. This time a lone protester came onto the field. He held up a sign that read, "Cuba, si; Castro, no."

How could this be happening here? Why couldn't they just play the game? Before they had left for Baltimore, Fidel had invited the entire team over to the presidential palace in Havana, not too far from the Habana Libre, where he and Pilar had honeymooned. Fidel had been all smiles and talked of baseball. He had warned Omar and the others to watch out for Mussina's knuckle-curve. Even *El Jefe* thought Baltimore would pitch its ace. He had reminded Omar to shake Cal Ripken's hand. How Ripken was a great ballplayer. No doubt Fidel had watched Ripken many times on his precious satellite TV. But even Fidel couldn't have foreseen how much of a circus this game in Baltimore would be. When the Orioles played in Cuba, there had been none of this madness. The crowd was mostly party regulars and sports federation people. True, the *Gran Stadium* wasn't as loud as usual. No salsa band or team cheers, but nobody had been so impolite as to run on the field and interrupt play, either.

For some reason, this protester was allowed to parade around the infield, holding up his sign. As he drew closer to second base, Cesar Valdez, one of the three umpires who had accompanied the team from Cuba, had words for him. The two of them—umpire and protester—began to argue.

"Get him, Cesar," shouted Jorge, the Cuban trainer, and it was as if Valdez somehow heard him above the growing din because the umpire amazingly grabbed the protester and started to wrestle him to the ground. As the crowd roared, security guards ran onto the field and Orioles outfielder B.J. Surhoff was the first player there, trying to pull them apart.

Omar turned to Morales and said, "Let's beat them so bad that they'll never forget us."

***

In the end, Morales did a better job than Omar of defeating the major-league Orioles. In the ninth inning, Morales hit a three-run home run. Almost an unbelievable feat considering he had only been swinging a wooden bat less than a month.

After Morales' drive cleared the green-colored fence in left-center field, the Cuban team stood on the top step of the dugout and applauded. The ballpark was already half-empty as Morales circled the bases like a drunken fool, laughing and holding his arms out, pretending to be an airplane. Team Cuba had proven that it could beat major leaguers. Never again would its players have to listen to the Yanqui sportswriters, the ones who steal onto the island to write about baseball in the socialist state. Never again would they have to listen to them pass judgment on Cuban ball. That a batter like Morales could, perhaps, play in the American Triple-A leagues. That a few of them, like Omar Silva, could reach the major leagues.

Hours later, in the hotel, Omar sat on the balcony and looked over Baltimore's harbor. With the uproarious crowd gone, the city settled into being a tranquil, almost lovely place. The reflections of the neon lights from the restaurants and tall buildings danced on the dark water like so many broken promises. Off to the left was Camden Yards, where they had played earlier that evening. Omar had been told that it was one of the most beautiful ballparks in the major leagues, and he saw now that it was true. The lights above the outfield seats were still on and he could see the outline of the ancient red-stone warehouse that overlooked the field. He could slip outside and reach that place in minutes, and the Orioles would take him in. He had proven himself tonight. He could leave and Pilar would someday follow. That was what she truly wanted, wasn't it? That's what she had whispered to him the morning he left for the special training camp at Pinar del Rio. How she wanted so much to live in this land. How she would find a way to follow.

There was a knock at the door and Omar opened it to find Jorge Gonzalez, the team's trainer. Jorge's breath smelled of rum and he was quiet, almost embarrassed to have disturbed the star player.

"Jorge," Omar said and held the door open, inviting him in.

The trainer barely came up to the player's shoulder. He shuffled into the room, eyes focused on his feet. Omar nodded toward the mini bar. "Drink?"

Jorge shook his head and held up a half-full bottle of rum.

"Here, sit down," Omar said and they settled into the two chairs on the small balcony overlooking the harbor and the ballpark. The night air was humid, like back home, but a hint of a breeze somehow reached them, even up there, high above Baltimore.

In the silence, they gazed upon the water and the city. At the ballpark, the huge banks of lights above the outfield seats went out section by section.

"Carmelo is gone," Jorge said. His voice broke and Omar feared that his friend was about to cry.

"He slipped away while everyone was celebrating downstairs," Jorge continued. "Even Contreras was there. The whole team except for you and Carmelo."

Omar tried to smile at this. Joke about it, but no words came.

"So when I heard he was gone," Jorge said, "and nobody had seen you…"

"You decided to check on me."

"No, it's not like that, Omar. It's just that if you had left, well, I don't know what I'd do."

Omar glanced again at the Camden Yards ballpark in the distance. Except for the flashing red lights atop the stadium and the white street lamps, it had faded into shadows and dark silhouettes. Still, it remained so close he felt as if he could reach it in one big step. Simply leap from this balcony and come down magically upon that glorious emerald field once again. He could do it and nobody could stop him. Jorge wouldn't dare.

"Have you ever thought about leaving?" Jorge asked.

Omar turned toward him, wondering if the trainer could somehow read my mind.

"I'm sorry," Jorge said. "I don't know why I came up here. Nobody ordered me to find you. You may think that's a lie, but it's true. I just had to see for myself because if you hadn't opened the door I would have gone back downstairs and gotten a whole bottle to myself. I wouldn't have told a soul. You can trust me, Omar. It's just that I don't know what I would do if I couldn't watch you play anymore."

Now it was Omar who struggled to find the right words. He reached over and clasped Jorge on the shoulder. He pressed hard, feeling the knots of muscle in the shoulder and upper back. Then Omar got up and walked over to the mini bar. He opened the dark-wood doors and found a bottle of scotch. He held it one huge hand, just staring at it. He knew this would cost him plenty in U.S. dollars. Omar held it another beat longer in his throwing hand and then proceeded to break the seal. He found two glasses in the bathroom and filled each halfway. One for Jorge and one for himself.

Back out on the balcony, they drank and gazed anew at the sleeping city. It had grown so quiet that they could hear the music and laughter from the hotel bar many floors below them.

"Those Orioles had a great third baseman," Jorge said.

"Where? Nobody on their team was much good."

"No, not now, but years ago," Jorge said and took a long sip. "Before the game I had to go over to their clubhouse. We didn't have enough tape or wraps. We never have enough. But their trainers were kind. They gave me plenty. One of them knew some Spanish and we got to talking. You should see their clubhouse, Omar. It is like a palace, with carpet and music speakers and more whirlpools than we have in our entire league."

"Sounds like you should have stayed there, Jorge," Omar replied. "Capitalism agrees with you."

Jorge shook his head. "No, no, Omar, it's not like that. I'm just telling a story."

"All right then," Omar said, sorry that he had embarrassed his friend. "Tell me."

Jorge nodded—eager to continue.

"In their clubhouse, there are large photos, like old movie posters," he said. "We stood in front of one of them and I asked who it was. They told me it was somebody called Brooks Robinson. They told me that Robinson played third base and once was even in our old winterball league."

"Robinson must be an old man by now."

"Yes, but he was the best third baseman they ever had with the Orioles. The trainer, his name was Mickey, said that Robinson won more Gold Gloves than he could remember and he could hit the long ball, did it with men on base and the pitcher bearing down. He was one of the best third baseman of all-time. And then do you know what he told me, Omar?"

"No," Omar replied. He didn't want to hear the rest, but he knew there was nothing he could do to stop his friend now.

"He said that you're better than Brooks Robinson," Jorge said, the words tumbling out. "Even though Mickey has barely seen you play, he says you're the best third baseman he's ever laid eyes on."

They finished their drinks in silence, watching the city settle into a deep slumber. After awhile, Jorge got up and patted Omar lightly on the back and then he headed for the door.

As dawn bled across the morning sky, Omar packed his things

in the old leather suitcase that had been his grandfather's. The story was that his grandfather had bought the suitcase from a salesman on the sidewalk in Coral Gables back in the day when a Cuban could take the ferry to Florida any time he wanted. His grandmother had told her husband that he was being foolish. That anything not from a store wouldn't last. But the Florida suitcase was still the best bag that the Silva Family had ever owned.

Omar carefully folded his clothes and began to tuck them away. The team bus left for the airport and the return flight to Havana at 7 a.m. After he folded the last shirt and put it in his grandfather's bag, Omar looked out the window at Camden Yards, home of the Baltimore Orioles. Downstairs he knew that Rene Tovar and other agents would be waiting, watching his every move. Yet as Omar closed the hotel door, he told himself to keep his eyes straight ahead once he got downstairs. File on to the bus with his teammates and Jorge and the others, and try not to look back at that beautiful ballpark ever again.

TWELVE

T HAT NIGHT, BEFORE THE LATE SHOW, Luz saw the Revlon lipstick from the Loot Party. It stood on end, like an attentive solider, again on her dressing counter. She looked around her, but there was nobody there. The other girls had already moved backstage, ready to go on. Alongside the golden cylinder was a small note from Elena. "It looks better on you two," it read.

Luz held the scrap of paper in her hand for a moment and then crumpled it up, throwing it half-heartedly at the waste basket. There was no "you two" anymore. News of Pilar's disappearance had undoubtedly swept through the working ranks of Cayo Coco.

Luz picked up the lipstick of muted pink and turned it in the strong light that emitted from the banks of bright-white bulbs that lined the edge of a large rectangular mirror. Had Pilar left for more of this? It had always been the United States with her best friend. If Luz had a coin for every time Pilar talked about when the embargo ended, when people could travel, well, she'd be rich. That Uncle Luis played along with such talk was too much. He even talked about going with her when that marvelous day arrived. But Pilar's Uncle Luis would have returned to Cuba. Luz was pretty sure she would have, too.

A stagehand opened the dressing room door.

"Luz, they're waiting for you," he said. Beyond him she heard the swelling of the house band and Jorge and Livan chattering to another big crowd.

Luz studied her reflection in the large mirror and brushed a strand of hair behind her hair. Her hair was thick and matted easily—not soft as silk like Pilar's.

As Luz hurried to the door, held open by the stagehand, she realized she still held the cylinder of lipstick in her hand. Pausing at the threshold, momentarily uncertain what to do, she flipped it toward the wastebasket. It rattled off the rim and spun to the floor. But Luz was already hurrying toward the stage, anxious to be in place when the curtain rose again.

THIRTEEN

T HEY AWOKE WITH A HOT, MID-DAY SUN OVERHEAD. Groggy, as if they were coming up from a bad dream, they took inventory of what had happened. One of the Hobie's hulls was submerged, an angry gash in its side. The other hull appeared to be undamaged and they sprawled awkwardly on what was left of the canvas deck, riding barely above the warm water. The food was gone. So were the water jugs. But Pilar had hung onto the compass and Pablo's small knapsack, the one with the Cayo Coco logo of a sun riding the horizon, somehow hadn't been lost to the sea. As Pilar watched him, Pablo dug into the cream-colored bag and came up with the book from the Loot Party. The way he held it, so tenderly, angered Pilar.

"A book?" she said. "What good is that going to do us now?"

He didn't have the courage to look her in the face when he replied, "Maybe I could read some of it?"

"Read it? Like aloud?"

"Yes," he said in a soft voice. "To both of us."

"Your English isn't good enough," she complained, eager to hurt him.

"I know enough," he said. "My father taught me. He had a gift for language."

Pilar looked about them and saw nothing but water. Flat and serene and spent after how it had taken advantage of them. The sharks would come soon. She didn't know much about the sea, but she was sure of this.

She reached for the compass—her keepsake from their survival. It was wedged in the front pocket of her cutoffs, and the only way she could pry it free was by undoing the top button. Pablo watched her with wide eyes as she struggled to get a better grip. Finally, she held the compass out in the palm of her hand and saw that north, to the United States, was actually behind them. They had gotten all twisted around in the storm and both of them peered over their shoulders as if the United States was right there, waiting for them. But, of course, there was nothing but water and the wide horizon. They would have to rig up some kind of sail. Something to keep them from the mercy of the current, which was taking them God knows where. But that would have to wait. They were both too tired to think straight in the heat.

"So, go ahead," Pilar told him. A tremor in her voice betrayed how brittle she felt, how quickly she could become scared out here, with nothing around them. "Read it, if you want. I don't care."

The boy began to read the soaked pages. His English was better than expected; though he had to skip a word here and there that he didn't know. Other times he paused, everything quiet except for the lapping of the gentle waves on the remaining hull, until he guessed at the translation. It was so quiet at such times that it was like they could almost make out the music and the buzz of conversation from the afternoon show at Cayo Coco. Both of them could almost imagine such times, never to be relived again.

When Pablo began again, he told the tale of a man named Sal Paradise and his friend Dean. How fast they talked and how they crisscrossed America—almost mocking how slow they bobbed about on what was left of the Hobie. Pilar began to drift off, almost asleep. The halting cadences of the boy's voice stole into her head and took on a life of their own.

"... the only people for me are the mad ones," Pablo read, "the ones who are mad to live, mad to talk, mad to be saved, desirous of everything at the same time, the ones who never yawn or say a commonplace thing, but burn, burn, burn like fabulous roman candles exploding like spiders across the stars and then in the middle you see the blue centerlight pop and everybody goes, Aww.'"

"Read that again," she asked, not opening her eyes.

Pablo repeated the passage and as he did so Pilar curled up next to him. She could hear the beating of his heart and the hoisting of his breath—ghost rattles in the chest. She slid one hand inside his shirt, letting it rustle what few chest hairs he had.

***

In the late afternoon, they awoke again—hungry and determined to do something about their deteriorating situation. In short order, Pablo found what was left of the smaller sail, the jib, curled up into a nasty ball beneath the submerged left hull. Together they pulled it up to the surface and there in the middle, with the fabric twisted about it, they saw the upper half of the aluminum mast. In the storm, when they had capsized, they had run over and crushed much of what was of use to them—the sails, the mast, all of the wire shrouds and lines. Pablo located a few stray tentacles of rope and saw what must be done. They set the broken mast atop the Hobie's good hull and hoisted aloft what they could of the small sail.

As soon as they erected the invention, they felt themselves begin to move through the water. Their progress was agonizingly slow. Nothing like it was before the storm. They had to shy into the building waves like an old man with a bad limp. The water ran across the canvas deck and they scrambled to the right-side hull, the good one, as they slowly picked up speed.

"The compass," Pablo said. Pilar pulled it free from her shorts pocket.

In the fading light, they both peered down at it.

"Almost," Pablo whispered and pushed what was left of the rudder away from him.

Slowly, the Hobie fell off the wind and slowed to a crawl.

"What are you doing?" Pilar cried.

"Pilar, it's okay. We're still moving."

Pablo took her hand and led it down to the water. He was right. They were moving. Barely.

"It's okay," he repeated as if he could read her mind. "Now we're going in the right direction."

The sun set in a hurry. It had given them enough daylight to finish their business and now it rushed to bear witness to the other side of the world. The light faded away but not before they glimpsed dark shapes out in the water, fins drawing closer, curious and beginning to circle.

"As long as we're moving, they'll leave us alone," Pablo said.

"How do you know?"

"That's what Señor Pena once told me."

Soon the darkness crept in from all sides, and the sharks and everything else disappeared until it was the two of them and what was left of the boat. Much later, Pablo nudged Pilar awake with an excited hand. The compass had served them well. There, rising out of the northern horizon, barely visible, were dots of light.

"God bless," Pilar murmured.

The lights were like giant arms waiting to hug them to its chest. For a moment, Pablo could believe that it would be this easy. That the great and rich United States of America would simply leave the door ajar and they would be able to steal in like beggars in the night. But then he saw the large boat far off to starboard. At first he tried to pretend that it was a large building, seen from a vast distance. Nothing more than that. Yet, as the two of them studied it, there was no mistaking that this bank of lights was moving toward them.

Pablo stood and began to wave.

"You fool," Pilar said and pulled him down. "What if it's their police?"

"So?"

"If they catch us at sea, they'll send us back to Cuba. We have to make land. Only then can we stay."

Pablo peered into the dark waters around the Hobie. He didn't see any fins, but the sharks were still out there. He was sure of it.

A searchlight from the Coast Guard vessel began to ply the surface and it soon fastened upon their small sail. Then it dropped lower and blinded them with its glare.

"Go," Pilar said and she fell backward into the sea. She pulled the boy in with her.

When they surfaced, the Coast Guard boat's motors revved and it hurried toward them.

They were maybe a mile or more from the shoreline. They would hunt in the waters between the Hobie and shoreline. Pilar was sure of it. So, she began to swim back out to sea, toward the deep water and the sharks. For the first time in weeks, the boy refused to agree with her. He pulled at her hand, wanting to go toward land. But she knew that way was no good. Pilar pulled back—hard—trying to tell him that this was their only chance. Pablo broke free of her grasp. That's when they heard the first of the announcements echoed across the water. The Coast Guard, in English and Spanish, warned them to give themselves up to the authorities. That was how Pilar lost Pablo.

***

The left side of her face was the first part of her body to reach America. Pilar washed up onto the beach in the dead hours before dawn. She could barely lift her arms as the waves pushed her farther up the beach. Only after a long while did she rise to a sitting position and looked around at where she had landed.

As her eyes focused, she saw figures that she first took for ghosts. They ran along the sand, so much in a hurry. They were dressed in shorts and white T-shirts with small reflectors on their shoes. Pilar watched them—fearful that she had gone mad.

Yet, it slowly came to her. These were joggers. Pilar had seen ones like this in the morning along the Malecon. They ran for their health. At least that's how it was explained to her once by somebody at the resort. Such craziness.

With difficulty, she stood and began to shamble after them. That morning near Key West, Florida, she was the slowest of the joggers in this new dawn.

FOURTEEN

"**H**E DIDN'T EVEN TRY."

"You don't know that for sure."

"Pilar, don't tell me what I know and what I don't know. We had every entrance to that hotel covered. The team was getting shit-faced in the bar and your Omar never came down. He drank the night away with the trainer up in his room."

Pilar looked out the window that faced the beach. It was one of the best views in the entire world. She had been told that and she now saw that it was true. The other side of the living room looked down upon the inland waterway that separated Miami Beach from the mainland. Through half-closed eyes what she saw below her could have passed for Cuba—Cuba with a lot more money. Enough cash for new paint, some kind of upkeep complete with shiny new cars that rolled across the glimmering asphalt streets.

Rene Tovar waited impatiently—his eyes followed her as she walked about the room.

"But you know, Rene," Pilar said, ready to face him head-on. "The more I think about it, I can't help thinking that you and your boys screwed it up."

"Careful, pretty one," he replied, refusing to be intimidated. "My company did well by El Duque and his half-brother. I've personally spirited more ballplayers out from under Fidel's nose than you can count on both hands and both feet. I can help Omar, but it's the same with every one of them. They have to make the first step."

"Maybe he didn't have the chance in Baltimore."

"Pilar, he had every chance in the world."

This Rene could seem like such a teddy bear, almost a baby Santa Claus, with his roly-poly build and his bright smile. But his dark eyes betrayed him. They could flash with so much anger.

"I waited all night in my car across the street from that damn hotel," he said, his voice a low growl. "He knew I was there. We took every precaution from calling his room to having Beatrice, one of my assistants, a beautiful girl, ask for his autograph down on the field before the game. She's supposed to be a TV lady. It's a great setup. Your Omar opened the leather notebook Beatrice handed him. It fell open to the middle, where he saw a picture of me, smiling at him. The message read that I was out there, waiting for him. All he had to do was give me a sign. Walk out of that hotel when everybody from his manager to security was shit-faced after their fucking win over Baltimore. All he had to do was take the first step. But your Omar never did."

Pilar didn't know what to say.

Rene smiled cruelly and added, "I swear one time that night I thought he was looking down on me. I was certain it had to be his room and he was up there. It was about three o'clock in the morning and that room was the only one lit up on the whole side of the building. I saw shadows out on the balcony. God, I was sure it was him. I almost got out of my car and went to wave up at him."

"I'm sure Omar still wants out."

"Well, Pilar, you better get to him somehow because right now you're the one living off such hopes and dreams. If Omar Silva doesn't defect, I don't see how I can keep putting you up in a place like this. It doesn't make any sense, does it?"

"Rene?"

"I'm serious, Pilar. You are a very resourceful woman and a true beauty. But right now the only hook you have in this country is that you're married to the best living ballplayer who hasn't signed a major-league contract. If he's decided to stay in Fidel's hell hole of a country, he doesn't do you or me any good."

Rene stood up and walked toward the door of the beautiful condo on Miami Beach. The kind of place where Pilar could live for the rest of her days if Omar ever joined her here in America.

Rene opened the door and glanced back. In an off-hand way, he said, "I found your little friend. The one who did have the balls to leave."

"Pablo?"

"He's locked up in Miami-Dade. He made the beach, too. You ran one way, he ran the other. He's got no family here in Florida. I wouldn't be surprised if they still try to ship him back to Cuba."

***

What they do in jails was lift the light out of your soul. That's what Uncle Luis had told her years ago. The uniformed officer looked down upon her from behind a wide counter. All around them snippets of conversation echoed through the cavernous reception hall under the fluorescent lights at the Miami-Dade jail. The uniformed man's English was so fast that Pilar felt as if she was back in the storm. All she could do was plunge in and hope the current carried her along.

"I'm his sister," she interrupted.

The officer crinkled up his nose as if he had smelled something bad. "He never said anything about a sister, or any family at all in the United States."

"I'm really a half-sister. I live near Tampa. We just got word that he had come here."

With a disgusted look, the officer flipped through the few slips of paper in Pablo's file.

The officer's name tag read Lester.

"Can I see some kind of ID?"

Pilar dug through her purse for the new Florida driver's license that Rene helped her obtain when she was still his link to Omar.

"Pilar Silva?" Lester said. "But his last name is Llanes. Pablo Ortiz Llanes."

"Like I said, I'm his half-sister. From what I've been told, that is good enough, right? All he needs is a sponsor for you to let him go."

Lester shrugged at this and continued to flip through the pages in Pablo's file.

"What does your Pablo Ortiz Llanes look like?" he asked.

"I don't really know. It has been years since I actually saw him. My family had old pictures of me—"

"You must have some idea. I mean how can I let him go with you if you don't really know?"

This was so stupid, so arbitrary. It was like something they would do back in Havana.

"C'mon, describe him."

Pilar closed her eyes and tried to picture Pablo that first day on the boat.

"He has dark eyes and short, wavy hair. His face could be a puppy's. He hasn't grown into it yet. To leave him in a place like this or to ship him back to Cuba would kill him."

Lester didn't answer and for a moment Pilar feared that she had gone too far. She watched as the man in uniform closed Pablo's file and tapped its spine once, twice, on the wooden counter top dotted with long scratches and deep gouges.

"Pull your car up front. I'll bring him out to you."

***

Pablo appeared, blinking in the bright sunshine. He studied the moonlight blue Honda that Pilar had stolen from Rene's fleet. She had packed up and driven it from the Miami Beach condo that morning. Maybe because Lester was still watching them, Pablo leaned over and kissed her on the cheek moments after he slid into the passenger seat. They were quiet as they sped away and into the spider's web of Miami's one-way streets.

"Where are we going now, Pilar?"

She didn't know how to answer him. How could she explain that she didn't really know? That the only thing she was certain about was that what lay out there, ahead of them, would be better than what they had left behind in Cuba. That she had believed such things for a long time and now was determined to make them so.

Pilar reached into the back seat. Atop the cooler was a plastic bag that crinkled to life as she brought it forward and set it on his lap.

He opened the bag from the bookstore and pulled out a new copy of *On the Road*.

"Pilar?"

"You'll need to read to me," she said. "We're going to be driving for a long time, several days I think. That's how far away Phoenix is from here."

"Phoenix?"

"A tourist told me about it once. How it's dry and hot. It's in the desert."

He gazed out the window, considering what Pilar had said and where they were headed.

"Why are you like this?" he asked, turning back toward her.

She accelerated into the left lane of the expressway leading out of Miami. Her driving was ragged, a bit fast, but he decided to believe that it would improve soon enough.

"I don't know," she replied, "but I can see them."

"Them?"

"The ones back home. That's what keeps me from going crazy. I think about what we're doing. As I once told you, I can imagine exactly what they're up to. I'm sure of it. It keeps them alive for me, helps me know that I will see them again, someday."

Pablo smiled at this. It sounded so crazy.

"Okay," he said. "What are they doing right now? Late afternoon on a Friday, the beginning of another weekend in Havana."

"I will tell you," she said. "Just close your eyes and listen."

FIFTEEN

MARIA WAS SPOONING THE LAST OF THE RICE and beans onto the dinner platter when she saw him coming up the narrow sidewalk from the street. Omar Silva was such a handsome man, lean and chiseled, and he moved in that peculiar way athletes do, like they are loose in the joints, so right with life. Jaime and Luis were already at the table. It was their Friday night dinner—a new ritual that had began for them in the weeks since Pilar's disappearance. They now gathered to compare news, of which there hadn't been anything conclusive, just more rumors. But it felt good to just be together. Sometimes, after the dishes had been cleared, with Jaime and Luis taking turns drying, they drove in Jaime's precious car down to the Malecon and gazed upon the Straits of Florida.

Maria opened the door before Omar had a chance to knock.

"Good evening," he said, almost embarrassed to be there, at his in-law's home.

"It's okay," Maria said and she held the door open. Behind her chairs scraped across the floor as her husband and his brother rose to their feet.

"Omar," Luis sang out. God bless him. Her brother-in-law could turn the most awkward moment into a celebration.

"I'm sorry it's taken me so long to come over," Omar said.

"Nonsense," Maria said and ushered him through the doorway and into the tiny dining room. Thankfully, Jaime remembered his manners and retrieved a folding chair from the closet.

Maria brought out another plate from the kitchen. One with the blue flower pattern that her mother had bought years ago, and just like that the best ballplayer in Cuba, technically still her son-in-law, was seated at their table. They passed him the rice and beans and the roast pork Luis had brought and the fried okra. For a moment nobody, not even Luis, was sure what to say, so they ate and nodded, simply happy to be in each other's company.

"It's good of you to come," Jaime finally began.

"I meant to come earlier," Omar said, his mouth half-full. He reached for his napkin and slowed to collect himself. "But one thing led to another. I've been trying to find out anything that I could."

"So have we," Luis said.

"But then, out of the blue, she called," Omar said, "less than an hour ago. I was lucky to catch her. I was going to practice."

"What did she say?" Maria asked, and for an instant she wanted to believe that her daughter was coming back to her. That it had somehow all been a big mistake. That even if she was swept up by the authorities that they had enough clout to get her out of any trouble she was in. Between Luis's connections, Omar's celebrity, they had easily more clout than they imagined.

"Pilar's in Phoenix," Omar said.

"Phoenix?" the rest of them replied. They had no idea where that was.

Already Jaime was going to the bookshelves for the old world atlas.

"It's in the United States, in the west," Omar said. "A long way from Miami, I believe."

Jaime brought the red-covered book with its gold-leaf pages back to the table and when he found the page they gathered around and peered down at the page for the state of Arizona.

"I know nothing about this place," Luis said.

"She said it's hot and dry," Omar said. "Several teams train there in the spring and the Diamondbacks are the major league club. That's all I know."

"But how did she end up there?" Maria wondered and Omar only shrugged.

"She and the boy—"

Jaime tapped the page absent-mindedly with his open palm. "She's still with the boy?"

"That's what she said. I don't really know why."

At the hint of loss in Omar's voice, Maria reached out to rest a hand on his shoulder. How could Pilar have left such a man, a man that loved her so?

"She has a job in a Spanish-speaking department store," Omar continued. "She wants me to come to her, but I don't see how that's possible. They're watching my every move now."

"Of course they are," Luis said. "They will be for some time."

They sat back down to dinner and Jaime placed the atlas, still open to the page for Arizona, on the end table near the television. Throughout the rest of the meal, each of them glanced at it, as if they were trying to understand how their beloved Pilar had ended up in such a land. Afterward, Omar took over for Luis in drying the dishes and Jaime got out the cognac and they sat on the back porch that faced the small garden. There was some conversation, but not that much. Instead they watched as the sky grew dark, happy to be in each other's company. Omar was the first one to leave, but not before Maria had packaged up a small helping of the roast pork and rice, and insisted that he come back again next week for dinner.

Luis was the next to beg off. It was a bit uncharacteristic for him to make an early evening of it, but he said there was plenty going on down at the garage and it promised to be a busy day there tomorrow.

Jaime tried his best to stay up with her. He began to talk in a voice a bit too loud for the hour about how he couldn't understand what Pilar had done. He was on the verge of getting pretty riled up until Maria leaned over and laid a finger across his lips.

"Hush, darling," she whispered. "It's over. What is done is done."

Jaime nodded.

"I can't think straight anymore," he said, standing up. "I'm going to bed."

So, Maria sat alone as the evening came on hard. So many questions and images rattled around in her head. She remembered a time, years ago, when they had thrown a party in this old house. Several of the people that Jaime worked for at UPI were there. Their home was packed to overflowing, and Pilar had been only two or three, yet she was so determined to stay up.

"She thinks she's an adult," Maria remembered Luis saying and she realized that it was true. That her daughter so wanted to be a part of everything. How she had cried when Maria took her up to bed with the party still going. Everybody was talking. A good half-hour after getting her down, Maria had crept up the stairs to check on her.

As she drew closer to Pilar's bedroom, Maria remembered she heard the most curious sound. It was the sound of skin hitting skin— a soft slap. As she looked inside the doorway, she saw her daughter, sitting defiantly in the middle of her crib. Poor Pilar was so tired. She could barely keep her eyes open. But, as Maria watched, she saw that every time the little girl was about to drop off to sleep, she reached up with an open hand and slapped herself lightly on the cheek. The shock was enough to keep her awake for another few moments, another sliver of time that she could hear the adults talking excitedly downstairs.

When her head drooped and she almost nodded off, again came the hand, slapping harder this time. It was the only thing that could keep her awake so she could hear more.

ACKNOWLEDGMENTS

THANKS TO GREGG WILHELM AT CITYLIT PRESS. He believed in this project and saw it through to the end. Chris Park paved the way so we could move ahead on all fronts, while Nathan Rosen did a great job on the cover and page design.

Alice McDermott read an earlier version of this story at the Sewanee Writers Conference several summers ago and she recommended that I "follow the fun" with it. In essence, focus on the characters that really resonated with me and see what they said and did next. I was fortunate to be a part of a great workshop in the Tennessee hills that summer, which included Greg Downs, Brendan Mathews, Michael Hyde, and Holly Goddard Jones.

Portions of this story appeared in *The Potomac Review* and *Gargoyle*. Thanks to Julie Wakeman-Linn and Richard Peabody, the editors at those fine publications.

Emily Williamson of Chrysalis Editorial was there to help me with the final edits and Paul White at *USA Today* made possible my first trip to Cuba back in 1992. I've since made several more trips to the island and have regularly counted on the expertise and insights of Milton Jamail, Bill Brubaker, Rick Lawes, Scott Price, Tom Miller, and Luke Salas.

The Writing Department at Johns Hopkins University continues to be my professional home. Thanks to David Everett, my students, and my fellow faculty members there.

As I write, the dysfunctional political relationship between the United States and Cuba has extended well into its fifth decade. Change is coming—someday. Anybody who visits the island can see that. But why wait any longer? Why not blow the trumpets and watch the wall between our two nations, real and imagined, fall away forever?

ABOUT THE AUTHOR

TIM WENDEL'S BOOKS include *Summer of '68: The Season That Changed Baseball, and America, Forever*; *High Heat: The Secret History of the Fastball and the Improbable Search for the Fastest Pitcher of All Time*; *Red Rain*; and *Castro's Curveball*. A writer-in-residence at Johns Hopkins University, his stories have appeared in *The New York Times*, *The Washington Post*, *GQ*, and *Esquire*. He lives in northern Virginia and can be reached at www.timwendel.com.

CITYLIT
PRESS

CityLit Press's mission is to provide a venue for writers who might otherwise be overlooked by larger publishers due to the literary quality or regional focus of their projects. It is the imprint of nonprofit CityLit Project, Baltimore's literary arts center, founded in 2004.

CityLit creates enthusiasm for literature, builds a community of avid readers and writers, and opens opportunities for young people and diverse audiences to embrace the literary arts. *Baltimore* magazine named the press's first book a "Best of Baltimore" and commented: "CityLit Project has blossomed into a local treasure on a variety of fronts—especially its public programming and workshops—and it recently added a publishing imprint to its list of minor miracles."

Thank you to our major supporters: the National Endowment for the Arts, the Maryland State Arts Council, the Baltimore Office of Promotion and The Arts, and the Baltimore Community Foundation. More information and documentation is available at www.guidestar.org. Additional support is provided by individual contributors. Financial support is vital for sustaining the on-going work of the organization. Secure, on-line donations can by made at our web site, click on "Donate."

CityLit is a member of the Greater Baltimore Cultural Alliance, the Maryland Association of Nonprofit Organizations, and the Writers' Conferences and Centers division of the Association of Writers and Writing Programs (AWP). The organization's offices are located in the School of Communications Design at the University of Baltimore (www.ubalt.edu).

For submission guidelines, information about CityLit Press's chapbook contest, and all the programs and services offered by CityLit Project, please visit www.citylitproject.org.

CPSIA information can be obtained at www.ICGtesting.com
Printed in the USA
BVOW082349040413

317355BV00004B/26/P

9 781936 328147